Libby's CUPPA Joe

A NOVEL

Rebecca Waters

Ambassador International
Greenville, South Carolina & Belfast, Northern Ireland
www.ambassador-international.com

Libby's Cuppa Joe

ISBN: 978-1-62020-867-0
eISBN: 978-1-62020-888-5
Library of Congress Control Number: 2019933627

Cover Design & Typesetting by Hannah Nichols
Ebook Conversion by Anna Riebe Raats
Edited by Katie Cruice Smith

AMBASSADOR INTERNATIONAL
Emerald House
411 University Ridge, Suite B14
Greenville, SC 29601, USA
www.ambassador-international.com

AMBASSADOR BOOKS
The Mount
2 Woodstock Link
Belfast, BT6 8DD, Northern Ireland, UK
www.ambassadormedia.co.uk

The colophon is a trademark of Ambassador, a Christian publishing company.

DEDICATION

For Tom

ACKNOWLEDGMENTS

My family continues to encourage me as I write. My mother reads everything. My daughters cheer me on. But it is my husband I need to acknowledge first and foremost.

Right after God, that is. God gave me the heart's desire to write. He gives me purpose and ideas. He gives me words and phrases, even when I think I have none left in me.

But Tom? My husband of forty-three years? When we decided to retire early, he was the first to embrace the idea I would write and publish. "You can do that," he told me.

He was the first to call me an author. He edited my drafts and read my manuscripts. For this book, *Libby's Cuppa Joe,* he tried everything I baked—from the breakfast cookies featured in the book to my first attempt at kringle, a delicate Danish pastry.

When my first book, *Breathing on Her Own,* was released in late March of 2014, Tom threw himself into creating a memorable book launch for me. We held it in the backyard of our lake home in Florida. Tom had the yard in perfect order and arranged tables and chairs and canopies to make the event festive and fun. He loved me. I can't imagine anyone loving me as fiercely as Tom Waters loved me.

Seven months later, he was gone. From this life, anyway. He had a bicycle accident. I lived in a fog for a very long time. But God is gracious and kind. He has awakened in me the desire to write again.

I praise God for my family, who continues to encourage me, and for a husband who had confidence in me. A special thank you goes to Cynthia Ruchti for her friendship and encouragement and allowing me to bring her into the story. I thank God for the people at Ambassador International who were able to see something of value in my work and have worked with me to bring this story to fruition. And I praise God for you, my readers. My prayer is that no matter what I say in these pages, you will hear what God needs you to hear.

PROLOGUE

A LUMP. AFRAID? MAYBE. A little. Mostly surprised. Libby didn't know anyone personally who had breast cancer. It wasn't that she was oblivious to the disease. More and more people were talking about it. Why, even last year, during the pumpkin festival, someone put together that Pink Peninsula 5K run. Everyone, it seemed, was wearing pink.

"Even the men!" Joe grumbled. Libby smiled at her husband's reaction to the bevy of pink-clad men wandering in and out of the coffee shop. It was only after he saw many of his beloved Green Bay Packers wearing pink socks that Joe changed his tune.

A lump doesn't necessarily mean I have cancer. I should have it checked, though. That much she learned from the anchor on the evening news. The pretty one with the long, dark hair. Libby couldn't remember her name. She saw her late one evening talking about early detection. A doctor demonstrated right on the television how a woman could examine herself. Joe walked out on that one, but Libby thought perhaps she should try it.

By the time she thought of it again, it was the middle of "the season." A lump was there, but it was small. It would have to wait. Vacationers from as far away as Chicago flocked to Door County in the summer months.

No, the high season was no time to travel to Green Bay. She could try to see Doc Burroughs but nixed the idea. Doc was a good one if you had a fever or broke a leg, but not something like this. Not woman stuff. There was a cancer center not so far away, but one of the Branson girls worked there. Wouldn't do to have her business spread all over the peninsula. Libby made a mental note to call her sister-in-law in Green Bay for a doctor's name. *Once the season's over, of course.*

And maybe, just maybe, she would consider retiring. Joe often talked of selling Libby's Cuppa Joe and moving somewhere where the weather was warm. Libby balked at the idea. Fish Creek, Wisconsin, was her home. More importantly, when their daughter, Judy, thought of home, she wouldn't imagine a condo on some golf course in Florida. No, Judy would want to come back to Door County, of that Libby was sure. But maybe after they dealt with this lump, maybe it would be time to consider moving on. They could buy a little retirement home somewhere close to family in Green Bay. *Maybe we could spend winters in Florida and summers in Wisconsin. Other people do it. Joe would like that.* Anything was possible. *After all, I'll be sixty-eight in a month, and Joe's already seventy-three. Perhaps this lump is a sign it's time to slow down. Once the season's over, of course.*

CHAPTER 1

SONJA PASSED THE FIRST THREE exits to Green Bay before pulling off the highway for gas. While it pumped, she called her best friend, Fran.

"I have this urge to get off the interstate and locate Happy Years Retirement Village. I would love to meet the previous owners. You know, I could assure them the business is in good hands."

"You're crazy. It's your business now. You don't owe them anything. You're just a pleaser at heart."

"Well, it doesn't matter anyway. I'm not going to go looking for the Davises on this trip. I may see how things go first."

"I still don't get why you'd leave San Diego for Fish Pond."

Sonja rolled her eyes. "Fish Creek, Fran. Fish Creek. And someday, when you get out of your little California bubble and visit, you'll understand."

"It must be some kind of Wisconsin thing. Anyway, I hope it works out for you."

Fish Creek. My new home. A home and a business—and before I'm thirty. Right on track. Sunshine flooded the small car, filling Sonja with warmth she never experienced on the California coast. *The warmth of home.* Sonja turned on the car radio for some soft jazz. *So different from four years ago when I was singing that old song, "California Dreamin'."*

Having grown up in Kenosha, Sonja longed for the lake. The ocean was beautiful, but Lake Michigan had the same mystery of unending water but without the salt. Sonja's parents were thrilled to see their only daughter return to Wisconsin and begged her to stay with them in Kenosha until school was out for spring break, when Annette, Sonja's mother, would be free to help her settle into the coffee shop apartment on the lower level of the building.

"It'll be perfect," Annette told her. "I can go with you when school's out for the week and help you clean everything and get it all set up. It'll be more fun than teaching second graders!"

Is it bad to want to be close to home but far enough away to do everything possible to avoid the whole "smother mother" thing? Sonja was anxious. "You can still come," she told her mom. "But I want to get started. You understand, don't you? Anyway, in a couple of weeks, I'll be back for that trade show in Chicago. I'll be staying with you then."

Now, pulling into the drive from the access road beside the wood frame structure, Sonja turned off her car's ignition and sat in the warm vehicle. She stared at the building, then closed her eyes, imprinting in her memory every detail of this moment. When she finally pulled the keys from the large envelope Susan had mailed her, she took a deep breath and walked to the front of the Victorian dwelling.

The porch was swept clean, poised to welcome customers. Sonja started to turn the key; but to her surprise, the door was already unlocked. Her heart pounded. She looked around. *No one nearby to call to for help.* Sonja retrieved her cell phone from her pocket, ready to dial 911 as she cautiously entered the coffee shop.

"Hello?" Sonja was surprised by the sound of her small, weak voice. *Certainly no way to scare off a prowler.* The front door opened into a large entry hall. Directly ahead, an expansive staircase led up to the large, spacious room on the upper floor.

Sonja willed her legs to move, but a chill ran up her spine. Perhaps it would be wiser to find someone, anyone, to enter the old building with her. Her thumb poised to push the emergency call button on her phone, Sonja walked slowly through the wide doorway on the right and entered the dining area. She made a quick sweep of the room. Shelves filled with books lined the walls on either side of the fireplace. Wooden tables and chairs of various sizes and styles were scattered throughout. No one was in this part of the building.

Clutching her phone and hoping she had cell phone service here, Sonja moved toward the kitchen. A scraping noise came from the living quarters below. Her heart beat rapidly as she walked through the kitchen to the back stairwell that led downstairs.

"Hello?" she called again, though this time with more confidence.

"Hello?" called a voice from below. Footsteps moved toward the stairway, and a woman's head appeared at the bottom of the staircase.

"Oh, hello there. You must be Sonja Parker," the woman said as she climbed the steep steps slowly.

"And you would be?" Sonja hesitated.

"I'm Joan Linder."

Sonja let out a deep sigh. "Oh, of course. The realtor told me you were going to turn on the water and all."

"Actually, my husband, Craig, did all that. I just came over to give the place a once-over."

"Uh . . . how nice." *A once-over?*

"Ms. Townsend said you would arrive today. I figured you would have enough to do, so I made a casserole so you wouldn't have to worry about dinner. 'Course if you have plans, it will keep in the fridge for a day or two."

"That was very kind of you." At the mention of food, Sonja realized she hadn't eaten since breakfast with her parents earlier that morning. "I take it you live near here?"

Joan Linder moved past Sonja toward the front window of the coffee shop dining area. She pointed toward the row of houses across the main road toward the water. "Just two houses past that blue one there on the corner's my place. My husband runs our bait and tackle shop there, and we live in the upstairs."

Sonja looked out the window but couldn't see the shop. On the main road, there were four houses directly across from her building. The blue house was a glassblower's studio. A potter lived next door. The third place of business was a candy store called Sweet Treats. That particular store had been in Fish Creek as long as Sonja could remember. As a child, she would beg for the sweet chocolate fudge she watched being made on the big slabs of cold marble in the quaint candy store. Sonja wasn't sure about the fourth building. It appeared to be someone's residence. It was surrounded by a white picket fence. There was no sign out front.

"Well, I guess I best leave you to settling in—unless, of course, you need help." Joan moved toward the front door.

"No, I'll be fine. I'll probably take a day or two to get settled." Sonja appreciated the woman coming but didn't relish the idea of someone she didn't really know helping her unpack.

"Well, if you need me, I left my number on your kitchen table. And my girl, Cassie, can help, too, if you have questions. She's sixteen. She helped Joe out last summer after Libby died, so she knows a lot about the place, too."

"What?" Sonja's mouth fell open. "Libby died? My realtor, uh . . . Ms. Townsend said they retired."

Joan looked past Sonja to the dining area. She bit her bottom lip. "Libby died of breast cancer last April. Joe tried to open up the shop in June, but his heart wasn't in it. He pushed through the season, but then he moved to some retirement home in Green Bay near his brother. That's why he sold the place."

Sonja gasped. The vision of the older couple happily living out their dream retirement—much like her Aunt Maggie and Uncle Russ were doing in Arizona—collapsed. She had convinced herself Libby and Joe had, in some way, hand-picked her to carry on the legacy of their coffee shop.

"Breast cancer?"

"She told me she found a small lump early but never had it checked because the season was upon us. I guess you realize how busy it gets in the summer here."

"I'm counting on it." *The season.*

So, Libby died of breast cancer. What else had the realtor not shared?

As Sonja unpacked her few things and prepared for bed that night, she found herself mourning the death of a woman she had never known. Sonja shuddered. *I should have asked Joan if Libby died at home or in the hospital.* She looked at the two bedrooms, one clearly the master and the other with a twin bed. She had sheets to fit both. It was her first night in her new home.

Sleep. I need to sleep! What's that noise? Ah . . . the refrigerator. Sleep, Sonja, sleep. Sonja looked at the time on her cell phone. *When will morning ever come?* The last time she noted was 4:24 a.m. before she finally drifted off to sleep on the lumpy, floral print couch.

CHAPTER 2

CASSIE ARRIVED ON THE DOORSTEP of the coffee shop promptly at four o'clock, just as Joan had promised. The sixteen-year-old looked nothing like her plump, brunette mother.

"My mom said you might need this." Cassie handed Sonja a copy of the school schedule. "I mean, if you want me to work here. I mean, if it's okay."

"Is it okay if I pay you what Joe was paying you?"

A smile spread across the girl's face. "Yes!"

"Then consider yourself hired. When can you start?"

"Whenever you need me, but it has to be in the evenings until school's out." Cassie motioned to the paper in Sonja's hand.

"Great. Then how about now? I could use some help in the kitchen."

"I'll have to call my mom."

Sonja took an immediate liking to the girl. After her call, the two headed into the kitchen.

"It was so sad when we heard Aunt Libby died in that hospital in Green Bay."

So, Libby had died at the hospital. Thank you, Lord. "I didn't realize Libby Davis was your aunt."

"She wasn't. All us kids just called them Aunt Libby and Uncle Joe."

"I see." Sonja stood at the door to the kitchen, her hands on her hips. "Well, I spent most of the day cleaning the apartment, unpacking, and exploring. I opened every cupboard, closet, and crawl space I could find. Now I'm ready to tackle the kitchen cabinets and pantry. You game?"

"Of course!"

Sonja and Cassie pulled tins, pans, pots, mugs, and plates from the tall cabinets lining the main floor kitchen. As they worked, Cassie told her new employer how Libby baked something every day.

"It isn't, or at least it wasn't, the kind of place where you go in and order what you wanted. You just ordered coffee or tea; and if you wanted a piece of whatever Aunt Libby made that day, you could get that, too. Say, what do you think this thing is?" Cassie asked, holding up a metal contraption with a long electric cord.

Sonja inspected it. The black cord was soft like fabric and badly frayed. The plug appeared to be porcelain. "I have no idea. I'm guessing it's some sort of kitchen appliance from the thirties or forties."

"We could plug it in and see what it does."

"Absolutely not. We'd likely burn down the entire building." Sonja took the piece from Cassie's hands and placed it in a box. *Better change the subject.* "So, what did Joe do for baked goods last summer?"

"Oh, he bought stuff from different people. Like, I think Mrs. Weaver baked coffee cake, and sometimes, we made cookies for him to sell. I would have baked cookies here, but he said no. My mom said the smell of cookies baking would make him sad."

"I can see that. So, Libby made cookies and coffee cake?"

"She baked all kinds of things. She would get up in the morning and say, 'This feels like a blueberry muffin kind of day, doesn't it?' And then she'd make dozens of blueberry muffins. Sometimes, she made pumpkin bread or blackberry bread. And she made really good cookies.

She always had cookies. My dad says Aunt Libby was the best baker in all of Door County."

The drawers revealed an assortment of eggbeaters, large spoons, and one incomplete set of aluminum measuring cups. There were no measuring spoons. Sonja concluded Libby was one who rarely measured the ingredients for her baked goods.

The rest of the contents were less intriguing. A final count revealed eight muffin tins of various sizes, six large cookie sheets, a variety of cake pans and pie pans, and eight loaf pans. Most were dented; and although they had been well-scrubbed, the aluminum pans had browned in the corners. In addition, two large, stainless soup kettles were part of the kitchen equipment. In one cabinet, they pulled out numerous saucepans and skillets. Glass and stainless bowls of all sizes were piled in one cabinet.

"But Libby didn't serve food here, right? Just cookies and such?"

"Most days, she made sandwiches for lunchtime," Cassie said. "If you came by around lunch, you could always get a peanut butter and jelly sandwich; and during the season, she had what she called a meat choice, too."

"What choices of meat?"

"No choices of meat, just a meat choice. You could get peanut butter and jelly or the day's meat sandwich."

"Oh, I see."

"There wasn't a whole lot of variety. She either made chicken salad, tuna salad, or egg salad. She called all of those meat sandwiches. But that was only during the season."

"And she did this every day?" Libby's Cuppa Joe was never going to be the same, despite her father's advice to maintain the status quo. No way was she going to run a restaurant.

"No, she didn't do it every day. If she had a lot of muffins or something left over, she didn't offer meat sandwiches. But you could always get peanut butter and jelly. And in the winter, she made soup."

"Well, I plan to close for the winter." Sonja looked to see how Cassie reacted to that bit of information.

"A lot of businesses here close for the winter," the girl replied without much emotion.

"Does your dad's business close?"

"Oh, no! Daddy would never do that. He sells mostly bait and tackle in the summer, but he sells stuff for ice fishing in the winter and has hunting stuff, too. We have camping equipment; and, well, we have everything outdoor sportsmen need in our store. And my dad can fix anything. You know, like fishing reels and stuff."

The young women pulled sixty-four ceramic mugs from the three cabinets above the pass-through to the dining area. There were several blue mugs of different shapes and designs and a number of plain white mugs that looked as though they had been purchased from a restaurant supplier. Twenty-nine of the mugs, however, bore the names and logos of a variety of businesses in Door County, while the remainder of the mismatched mugs were from differing cities, states, and vacation destinations. In the same cabinets, Sonja was pleased to find several unopened sleeves of disposable cups and lids. She knew there were two full boxes of the insulated paper cups in the walk-in pantry. Markings on the box indicated there were one thousand cups and lids inside each. It was a start.

The two were about to call the task done when Cassie pointed to the very top cabinet above the pantry. "I wonder what's up there?"

Getting the stepladder from the utility porch, Sonja gingerly handed down individual pieces of china. Lined up on the counter were sixteen china teacups and saucers, as well as three beautiful china teapots, each with matching creamers and sugar bowls.

"I've never seen those before," Cassie said as she admired the pattern of violets on the teacups.

Sonja turned a cup over. "Made in Occupied Japan. Hmm, I'll need to look these up when I try to figure out what that metal thing is."

The two carefully wrapped the tea sets in newspaper, placing them in a box that only this morning had contained Sonja's collection of sweaters.

"I'll look these things up on the internet as soon as I get service. The company is scheduled to come to the shop on Thursday the fifteenth."

She pulled out a pad of paper and added the china and unknown electric appliance to her growing list of information she needed as soon as she had internet installed. At the top of her list was the supplier the Davises had used for their coffee, and second on the list was "Get the address for Happy Years Retirement Village."

"Now what?" Cassie looked around the countertops and tables filled with everything that had once been in the kitchen cabinets.

"Well, I guess I'll make a list of everything here, organize it, and put most of it back. I just need to know what I have and where it is; so, if I need it, I can find it." She had no intention of baking as Libby had done, but there was no need to share that with Cassie. Specialty cookies and biscotti ordered from a company she found online would be one of the first changes she made to Libby's Cuppa Joe. *No need to toss all of the baking tins aside, though, until I'm sure of what I'm doing. It wouldn't hurt to maybe offer muffins on the weekends, especially if I can bake them ahead.*

After Cassie left, Sonja scrubbed all of the cabinet shelves and began organizing the items. As she put everything back into the cabinets and drawers, she had the strange feeling she was probably not changing anything from the way it had been when she started. The only real benefit was removing unnecessary clutter and knowing exactly what she had in her coffee shop kitchen.

In addition to disposable coffee cups in the pantry, there were only a few items on the shelves: an unopened tin of cocoa, a mason jar filled with nuts, and several cookbooks. On the floor near the back, she found cases of paper napkins, each imprinted with the name Libby's Cuppa Joe and the image of a steaming cup of coffee beneath the name. Sonja threw the nuts away, as she was unsure of their origin. She set the cocoa back on the shelf.

It was almost eight o'clock in the evening when Sonja stretched and headed down to her apartment for dinner. More chicken casserole. Joan was obviously used to cooking for a large family. If she planned it out and had the stomach for it, Sonja was sure the one casserole could feed her for the week.

"It's my meat choice," she said to herself with a laugh as she carried the cookbooks down to her lower-level apartment. *It's literally that or peanut butter and jelly.* She reached the bottom step as her cell phone rang.

CHAPTER 3

SONJA FISHED HER PHONE FROM her pocket. *Fran.* "Hey friend."

"Catch you at a bad time? Grinding beans or something?"

"No. Not yet." Sonja dropped the cookbooks on the table. "I've been cleaning all day, and I'm beat."

"Oh, the joy of owning your own business!"

"Yeah, well, what are you doing?"

"Just thought I'd check to see if you're getting settled in."

Sonja surveyed her living quarters. The real estate listing described the lower level of the coffee shop as a basement apartment. To Sonja, it looked more like a house. The entire back of the level opened out to the sloping backyard. A door led outside to a stone patio area. Large windows on the backside allowed natural light to fill the main living and kitchen area. The area was open and spacious. The two large bedrooms and a bathroom were located toward the front of the dwelling, and each had a small window located high on the wall.

"I'm getting there," Sonja said. "The furniture isn't as bad as I remembered from when I saw it in November. The furnishings are, for lack of a better description, eclectic."

"That can be cool."

"Yeah, but it wasn't put together in a way that made all the pieces work together as an interior designer might envision. Maybe because they packed up most of the personal items. There's one thing you'd love, though. A pillow with a picture of a hobo and the words 'Will work for coffee' embroidered on the front."

"Very funny."

"They left a floral print couch with an orange and brown crocheted afghan thrown over the back. Maybe that's more your style."

"Sounds like my grandmother's house."

"Totally. Complete with matching recliners and an old television."

"What are you going to do with all that junk?"

"Watch it, Fran. You're talking about my home here. Anyway, it's better than some of the furniture I had in college. There's some good stuff, too. There's a cool rocker in the bedroom. It's wood and sort of glides."

Sonja walked through each room as she described them. Both bedrooms were furnished with heavy pine furniture. Both had a dresser and a chest of drawers. The rooms were about the same size, but one had a full-size bed, and the other a twin. "I figure the one with the full-size bed is the master."

"So, is it creepy sleeping in some old woman's room where she died?"

Sonja sat down in the rocker. "Well, A—she didn't die here; and B—it's really a nice apartment. Bigger than any place I ever had before."

Sonja stood and inspected the nails on the wall above the dresser where several pictures or photos had been removed. "My mom's going to be coming up in a couple of weeks and help me paint everything. That'll put my stamp on it."

"Uh, not to change the subject, but uh, I saw Greg last night. He asked about you."

Sonja twisted a strand of hair around her finger. "So, what did you tell him?"

"I was cool. I told him you moved some time ago to Fish Tank."

Sonja rolled her eyes. "Creek, Fran. Fish Creek."

"Whatever. I told him it is a really remote place, and you couldn't be reached."

"Not that he ever tried." Sonja wanted to ask how he looked or if he was alone, but let the topic fade. The conversation turned quickly to work at ADK Logistics and their boss, who insisted on keeping the thermostat at sixty-eight degrees.

"You'd think we shipped frozen food out of here instead of bathroom fixtures."

"Tell me about it! That is one thing I do *not* miss."

"I thought people from Wisconsin love the cold."

"Sixty-eight degrees in Wisconsin calls for a picnic or day at the lake. It's just that I prefer the cool temperatures to be outside. Not inside my cubicle."

The conversation ended with a promise from Sonja to send a few pictures of the coffee shop. Sonja stretched her arms above her head and stood on tiptoe. She surveyed her apartment once more. *I didn't just buy a business; I bought a home as well.*

Sonja managed to push any thoughts of Greg out of her mind as she dished out a portion of Joan's chicken casserole and put it in the microwave. As her dinner warmed, Sonja sat down at the kitchen table to examine the cookbooks.

Three of the cookbooks were the kind that churches or community groups put together for fundraisers. Each entry had the name of the contributor beside it. Sonja flipped through the pages, hoping to find Libby Davis' name on one of the recipes. She slowed down and turned page by page through the sections marked "Cookies, Pies, and

Desserts" in the first book; Libby Davis' name was nowhere to be found. There were a few handwritten recipes on the inside cover. One was for coconut lemon bars and had the name Christy beside it. The other was a recipe for Jackie's Chocolate Breakaway Bars. Both sounded simple and delicious but expensive to make. *Not for a large number of people.*

When Sonja picked up the second cookbook, several pieces of paper fell to the table. Most were recipes. Some had a list of ingredients with a simple "mix and bake" written at the bottom. No clue was given as to what the recipe would make. Some of the recipes were written on index cards; but most were on envelopes, the corner of a paper placemat, or a napkin. A few had been torn from magazines.

Among the papers, Sonja found a thank you note from someone named Barbara. The precise, scripted handwriting spoke of a time when handwriting was taught almost as an art in school. Sonja's grandmother had demonstrated the same graceful lines in her own hand. Apparently, the Davises had given Barbara and her new husband, Ralph, an "exquisite tea setting" they would "enjoy for years to come." She promised to think of Libby and Joe every time they used the set. She had also included the recipe for the wedding cookies "for Judy," trusting that when the time came, they would be able to return to Door County to see her walk down the aisle. "Judy?" *Did the Davises have a daughter?*

Sonja pulled the recipe from within the fold of the card. Wedding cookies. Grandma Grace made wedding cookies from time to time. She promised when the time came, she would make them for Sonja's wedding. Sonja bit her lip and returned to her task, carefully putting the card and recipe back where she found it.

A black and white snapshot of two teenagers was tucked in the back of the third cookbook. The boy was standing on the side of a docked fishing boat. The girl was standing on the dock holding a string of fish. The young couple looked to be sixteen or seventeen years old. Sonja wondered if it was a picture of Libby and Joe. Maybe they had two children. Or maybe it was a picture of Judy with her boyfriend. Sonja turned the picture over, looking for names. Scrawled on the back were the words "Perfect day." Whoever the boy and girl in the photo were, they were happy. Sonja slipped the photo back into the cookbook.

A large plastic bag stuck out from the confines of the only large hardcover cookbook in the bunch. All the warranties and instruction manuals for every piece of equipment in the coffee shop kitchen were stuffed inside. They were current and matched the inventory Sonja had found in the work kitchen.

She picked up the instruction manual for the coffee brewing system set up in the upstairs coffee shop kitchen. The purchase papers were inside. The brewing system looked new. The papers revealed the centerpiece of her kitchen was only two years old. Cassie said Joe opened only on weekends that last season, so the hours on this brewer had to be low. Sonja was about to put everything back in the bag when a handwritten note on the front of the instruction manual caught her eye.

"Coffee: 3CCR for every 1CFCR

3pslt LRG or one pslt S"

Sonja ate her chicken casserole as she read the manual from cover to cover. It would be good to know how to use the machine; but more importantly, she hoped to find information to help her decode the cryptic message on the front cover. Could it be a recipe for making coffee? If so, she may never know what made Libby's coffee so special.

CHAPTER 4

THE FIRST WEEK AS THE proprietor of Libby's Cuppa Joe went by quickly as Sonja scrubbed every visible inch of the main floor of the coffee shop. At least three mornings, two or three people showed up expecting the place to be open for business. Finally, she locked the door and ignored the insistent knocking. *Locals! Humph!*

Sonja scrubbed her living quarters as well, boxing up the unwanted farm picture and afghan with odd items from the kitchen. *I'll give those to a thrift store or something.* On Saturday, she went to a grocery store called Main Street Market she found in Egg Harbor and purchased sandwich makings, cereal, a few vegetables, and fruit. She also bought several cans of ravioli, a box of spaghetti, and two cans of spaghetti sauce. *Joan's warmed-over casserole, a box of pop tarts, and Ramen noodles were fine for a few days; but now that I'm settled, it's time to cook.* "If you can call heating up a can of ravioli, cooking," she muttered to no one in particular.

After putting the groceries away, Sonja gave herself the rest of the day off. She donned her jacket and headed out to explore Fish Creek. The curtains on the house next to the candy store fluttered for a brief moment as she crossed the road. Sonja had the feeling she was being watched. She made her way past the blue house. Rounding the corner and heading down the side street toward the water, Sonja immediately spotted Dewey's Bait and Tackle. A tall, skinny man with hair pulled back in a short ponytail sat on the front step. He held a fishing pole on his lap and appeared to be carefully wrapping colored thread around the pole in an intricate pattern.

"Hello there," Sonja said.

The man looked up, "Hello there. You must be Miss Sonja." He had the same engaging smile and light brown hair of his daughter.

"And you must be Craig Linder."

"Yep. Nice to meet you," Craig answered as he stood to greet his new neighbor.

"Thank you for opening up the coffee shop for me. So, who's Dewey?" Sonja asked, pointing to the sign.

"My daddy and my granddaddy. Both were named Dewey. But my mother said no to naming me Dewey. She wanted something more *refined*." Craig said the word "refined" as if it were a family joke. Sonja looked the man over. No, he was far from refined but a good man with a good sense of humor.

"Is Joan around?"

"Inside, I think." Craig sat down and returned to his task.

Sonja stepped past him and entered the bait and tackle store. *Cassie was right. This store has everything.* A rack holding at least fifty fishing rods stood toward the back of the store. To her right were shelves of fishing lures and tackle boxes. Spools of fishing line, like ribbon in a sewing store, were displayed on a rack above a table of miscellaneous items marked with a cardboard "Clearance" sign on it. Every shelf and rack were full to overflowing.

Orange life vests hung on hooks from the ceiling. Various nets hung on the walls. Immediately to her left was a glass display case that ran along the front wall. A service counter, complete with an old cash register, stood out from the wall on the left. Another glass display case butted against the service counter. She didn't see any guns but noticed a locked case on the wall behind the service counter marked "Ammunition."

"Joan?"

"Under here," came Joan's muffled voice.

Sonja rounded the corner of the glass case, noting the knives of all sizes and colors displayed there. Joan was on her hands and knees, her head to the floor looking under the case. She raised herself up from the wood floor, triumphantly holding a Star Wars figure in her hand.

"Sorry about that. Cody, our youngest, lost his Darth Vader under the showcase."

"I haven't met your boys yet, though Cassie's told me about them."

"Oh, I'm sure Cassie had a lot to say," Joan said as she rolled her eyes. "She's the oldest, and her brothers bug her to death."

"Actually, she speaks fondly of them." Cassie did speak lovingly of her two siblings. *Most of the time.*

"Well, that's good." Joan seemed relieved. She invited Sonja to the back of the building, where she offered her tea. "I don't have any cookies or anything. Those boys of mine eat like there's no tomorrow."

"Oh, I'm fine. I just decided to take a break from everything and explore the town a bit."

"Hold on a minute," Joan told her as she slipped back into the storefront. She returned carrying a tourist map of Fish Creek. "Now this here is an old map, but nothing really changes. The new map will come out next month, and you'll get some for the coffee shop. But until then, this should help you figure out the lay of the land, so to speak."

Sonja studied the colorful map. The sides advertised various stores and sites. She noted Dewey's Bait and Tackle had a small ad in the corner, but no ad for Libby's Cuppa Joe could be found on either side of the promotional map.

"Libby's never needed to advertise," Joan told her, as if reading her mind.

Joan pointed out several places on the map, telling Sonja which businesses or families were seasonal and closed for the winter and which ones she'd find open. She told Sonja about various lighthouses nearby and the Peninsula State Park. When Sonja asked where she might find wireless internet service, Joan pointed to the library/post office on the map.

"Of course, the library part is only open three days a week right now. During the season, they'll be open every day, except Sunday, of course." Joan folded the map and handed it to Sonja.

The two women talked as they sipped their tea. Joan had married at nineteen and had her first child at age twenty. That made her thirty-six. *Not that much older than me.*

Sonja liked Joan. She liked the whole Linder family. She hadn't met the boys yet but knew instinctively they would be fun, full of energy, and interesting.

Picking up her map, Sonja said her goodbyes and set off on her walking tour of the immediate streets near the coffee shop. She walked all the way to the marina before turning to head home. *Home*. The word sounded good. Sonja was beginning to feel this place truly was destined to be her home.

Twilight was upon her as she crossed the road to Libby's Cuppa Joe. She shot a furtive glance toward the house with the picket fence. Was someone watching her as the sun disappeared behind the trees? Sonja quickly slipped into the front door of her new home. *What an uneasy, uncomfortable feeling.* Uneasy was the right word. Not frightened. *Still, it would be a good idea to meet more members of the community—starting with the neighbors.* Perhaps she would even learn who lived in the little house across the road. Until then, she bolted the door.

CHAPTER 5

"YOU MUST BE THE NEW owner of Libby's," the young woman at the library desk noted when Sonja asked about internet access on Monday afternoon.

Sonja was quickly learning everyone in Fish Creek knew who she was. She was also learning everyone referred to the store she now owned simply as Libby's. She had introduced herself to the young couple from The Potter's Wheel on Sunday afternoon. They, too, had greeted her with a "You must be the new owner of Libby's."

"I'm Sonja," she said, her hand extended in friendship.

"I'm Rose." Rose's hair was long and pulled back loosely in a ponytail. Wisps of her fine, blonde hair escaped the elastic holder, framing her face. Her smile was genuine. Sonja guessed her to be in her mid-to-late twenties. Rose led Sonja to a counter where four desktop computers were set at the ready.

"Oh, I brought my laptop," Sonja informed the young librarian.

"No problem. We have free wireless. Did you want to get a library card?"

I wonder if getting a card is required to use the wireless. It wasn't that she was opposed to getting a card; she was merely anxious to get started on her work. Sonja twisted the strap on her laptop case.

"Sure." Sonja filled out the form Rose placed in front of her.

"It'll be ready in a minute. If you want to do your internet stuff, feel free to sit anywhere. I'll type this in and have your card here when you leave."

Sonja looked around the room. She was the only patron. The library was small—much smaller than the branch library she used in Kenosha—and even that library she considered tiny compared to the one she enjoyed in San Diego. This library was, in fact, an extension of the town's post office and tourist information center. There were open tables in the middle of the room. Sonja started toward the one farthest away from the desk where Rose worked but thought it might send a message that she was unfriendly. She moved to the second table and unloaded her laptop from the case.

Looking at the list in front of her, she knew she should take care of business items first. She wanted to contact the coffee supplier the Davises had used and order the specialty cookies she had researched earlier. She decided to check her emails first.

She searched her inbox. Confirmation for the trade show near Chicago was there. She clicked on the link to the website and reviewed the program offerings. It would be good to attend the four-day show, take in the lectures, meet with suppliers, and investigate the new coffee equipment available. The show was a little over an hour drive from her parents' home in Kenosha, just a bit over the Wisconsin-Illinois line. The plan was to stay the nights with her parents and make the drive each day to the event.

The trade show opened a week from Wednesday. Leaving early on Tuesday allowed time for her to stop at Happy Years Retirement Village to meet Joe Davis on her way to Kenosha. She looked down her "To Do" list and circled the item "Find Joe's address."

Amy, a friend from college, sent two chatty emails. There was also one from her friend, Fran, as well, inquiring how everything was going. She responded quickly to both, giving each a brief description of the work she had put into the coffee shop so far. "Spent two days scrubbing all of the floors and woodwork," she read as she typed. "Dusted all the books and games and went through all the games to make sure all the pieces were there. They aren't." She explained she wouldn't have internet for another few days.

There was an email from the electric company welcoming her as a customer and explaining the online payment service they afforded customers. A message from Susan Townsend, her realtor, welcomed her to Door County. She smiled as a new message appeared. It was from the Door County Library. Sonja looked at Rose.

"I take it my library card is ready," she said to the young librarian.

"I feel silly asking you this, but would you like a cup of coffee?" Rose asked.

"That would be great. Why would you feel silly?"

"You own a coffee shop! Just be prepared for a regular cup of coffee. Nothing spectacular."

Sonja crossed over to the counter and followed Rose into a private office just off the main room. A small coffee pot on a table in the corner held the warm brew in a glass carafe.

"I have a confession to make," Sonja offered. "I'm just learning this business. I'm certainly no pro."

"You're so brave. I mean coming here and starting a business of your own and everything."

"It's just that I always wanted to own my own business. I have confidence I can make this work. I've done a ton of research."

"So, do you bake, too? I mean Libby always baked. It smelled so good when you walked in."

"I'll have cookies and such," Sonja responded vaguely as she returned to her desk. She enjoyed the aroma of fresh brewed coffee but had not considered how fresh baked goods also attracted customers. "Maybe some muffins on weekends."

"If you need help, I'm here," Rose said. "I usually walk to Libby's two or three times a week during the season. Sometimes, we get books returned to us that belong to Libby's; and every once in a while, people return our books to the coffee shop." The sound of a small bell above the front door of the library signaled the arrival of a new customer, and Rose excused herself to help an older gentleman holding an armful of books.

Sonja finished her cup of coffee thinking once again of the cookbooks on her kitchen table. It wouldn't hurt to make some sort of signature cookie during the week. Her mother used to make something she called "breakfast cookies." Sonja finished her coffee and returned to her computer. She sent an email to her parents, updating them on all she had accomplished and asking her mother if she still had the recipe for the breakfast cookies. As she remembered it, the cookie was perfect for dunking in coffee.

The next major item on her list was to find out where she needed to go to get her Wisconsin driver's license. The website revealed she needed to bring several documents with her, including her birth certificate and her current California license. The site had a list of possible documents she could use to prove she was a resident, one of which was proof of owning property. Being able to say she owned a home and business in Door County was like giving herself a generous hug. Sonja wrote the list in her notebook.

Facebook was a different animal. Sonja intended to set up her new store with an account but got caught up in reading all of the posts her friends and family had put up in the last few days. When she looked up, it was already after four o'clock. She packed up her things and invited Rose to stop by Libby's the following afternoon.

"I'll feed you a sandwich, and you can look at the collection of books there. I dusted every single one, but there is no rhyme or reason to the way they are organized."

"I'll be there! Like I said earlier, I will happily help you any way I can."

"I'm not asking you to organize them. Just give me some ideas. Besides, I don't know very many people yet. Actually, the only people I know at all are the people from Dewey's Bait and Tackle, really. I would welcome the company. Maybe you could fill me in on some of the people in Fish Creek." *Should I tell her I feel like I'm being watched, or do I sound like a weirdo? Maybe I'm just a paranoid city girl.*

CHAPTER 6

THE DRIVE TO GREEN BAY gave Sonja time to reflect on all she had accomplished in her first couple of weeks as the owner of Libby's Cuppa Joe. She had secured her Wisconsin driver's license, taken care of her insurance, ordered coffee, read the coffee maker manual from front to back twice and tried her hand at baking a batch of muffins from scratch under the watchful eye of her friend, Joan. She had also managed to clean the building from top to bottom, going through most of the storage areas piece by piece, and had made three trips to the thrift store in Egg Harbor with donations.

There was still a large attic area with numerous boxes neatly stacked under the sloping ceiling. The box closest to the door was filled with Christmas decorations. Sonja decided the rest of the attic treasures could wait.

Rose proved a great help with the books. She explained to Sonja how Libby's lending library worked.

"Libby told people if they found a book they liked, they could keep it and bring it back next year when they returned to Door County," Rose explained.

"I'm surprised there are any books left!" Sonja marveled.

"Are you kidding? People loved it. They would come back and bring extra books with them to donate. And if they didn't come back, they would often mail it back. Sometimes, they would put a book in the library book drop."

"Did they check out books from the library as well?"

"Oh, sure, sometimes. We let tourists get library cards; and they can borrow books, but not everyone knows that. Libby thought a cup of coffee and a good book go hand-in-hand, so she wanted to make sure books were available. And she always had Louis L'Amour on hand for Joe. I bet he read every Western story the man ever wrote at least twice."

Now, driving toward Green Bay, Sonja recalled the conversation and patted the three Louis L'Amour books on the seat beside her. Gladys, the name she gave to her GPS voice, guided her without problem through the streets of Green Bay to the Happy Years Retirement Village on the west side of town.

Happy Years Retirement Village was not a village at all, but rather two big brick dormitory-style buildings with a fenced courtyard separating them. Sonja parked in the lot designated for visitors and entered the first building through a glass door. The entry was wide and welcoming. She approached the counter and rang the bell for assistance. On the counter was a basket filled with red silk roses. Beside it lay a sign-in sheet for visitors. Sonja glanced at the sheet.

"Good morning! May I help you?" the young woman appearing behind the counter asked brightly.

"Oh, yes. I'm here to see Joe Davis," Sonja answered tentatively. "But I don't know his room number."

"No problem. I'll look it up." The attendant typed Joe's name into her computer. "Room 211. Through these double doors and down the hall to your left. Take the elevator up to the second floor, and it will be down the hall to your right. Just sign in right here, and I'll buzz you in."

Sonja signed her name to the clipboard as she rehearsed the directions given her. "Left, elevator to two, then right. Room 211." She smiled at the attendant and walked toward the doors. A buzzer sounded, and Sonja pushed the door open.

An odd odor greeted her as she stepped off the elevator onto the second floor. Several residents were gathered in a large, open area. Many were in wheelchairs. Several were using walkers. Some were sitting at tables playing checkers or cards. Others were sitting, staring out into space. As Sonja made her way past the group of elderly people, one woman looked up at her and reached for her arm.

"Oh, Debbie, there you are!" she said happily. An attendant rushed to Sonja's aid.

"Now, Miss Evie, this isn't Debbie. Debbie comes on Sundays. Remember?" Then, turning to Sonja, she said, "I'm sorry about that."

Sonja smiled weakly. "No problem." She moved through another set of double doors and down the tiled corridor until she reached room 211.

There were two beds in the room but only one occupant visible from the doorway. A man with gray hair sat in a wheelchair, his back turned to her and looking toward the window. He was wearing a dark blue sweatshirt and gray sweatpants. From the doorway, Sonja could see his left hand on the arm of the chair. The hand was big and looked strong. An attendant walked up behind Sonja as she hesitated at the door.

"May I help you?" the attendant inquired.

"I came to see Joe Davis."

The man in the wheelchair turned. "Judy? Is that you?"

Sonja walked into the small room. It reminded her of the hospital room her grandmother occupied the last days of her life.

"Mr. Davis? My name is Sonja. Sonja Parker." Sonja moved to where the man could see her.

"Sonja? Nice to meet you," he said, extending his hand.

"Uh, I, uh . . . I'm the person who bought your store," Sonja told him. She wanted to run away. *What am I doing here anyway?* This was not at all what she pictured. Did he even know the store had been sold?

"So, you bought Libby's." It was more of a statement than a question. Maybe he did know the place had been sold. He was looking at her now. Sizing her up, she suspected. "It's a good place, you know. Always been good to me."

Sonja wasn't sure what she should say or do next. She handed Joe the Louis L'Amour books.

"I understand you love Louis L'Amour. I found these three, so I brought them to you."

Joe accepted the books with a smile. "Can't read so good anymore. Diabetes keeps messin' with me. But thanks."

Sonja relaxed. Joe appeared to be in good mental health. She looked for a place to sit down. Pulling a small chair closer to Joe, Sonja asked if she could ask him a few questions about the business.

"Sure, I welcome the company. Always liked to talk about Libby's. Named after my wife, you know."

"I'm sorry I never got to meet her," Sonja answered honestly.

"She had a way about her, that's for sure. Always made people feel special." Joe smiled. "Yep, Libby's just wasn't Libby's anymore without her. I tried, you know. She wanted me to keep it going. Said that's where our girl, Judy, would always call home."

"I know you tried."

"But now there's you. You can keep it going. So what kind of questions did you have?"

"Well, I want to serve a good cup of coffee," Sonja began.

"Good idea, seeing it's mostly a coffee shop!" Joe laughed.

Sonja was beginning to feel more at ease. Joe was not in good health, but he had a good sense of humor. He was good with people. She could imagine him having coffee with customers, chatting and joking.

"I found what looks to be a recipe for coffee written on the cover of the instruction manual for the brewer, but I can't figure it out," Sonja said. "It says '3CCR for every 1CFCR'; and under that, it says '3pslt LRG or one pslt S.' Does that make any sense to you?"

"Not the way you're readin' it. Here, let me see that."

Joe took the manual in his left hand and brought it up close to his face, while with his right, he fished for a pair of glasses hanging around his neck on a cord. He moved his eyes over the cover through the thick glasses, adjusting the writing one direction or the other from time to time. He seemed to be studying each letter carefully. Sonja realized he was nearly blind. She was beginning to regret having brought this problem to him when he suddenly put the paper down.

"That's Libby's writing," he declared. "That's how she made coffee."

That much Sonja had figured out. She wasn't annoyed, though. Joe seemed so happy to see his wife's writing. Sonja could imagine Libby experimenting with the new coffee maker, trying the best combinations to perfect her brew. She could imagine her predecessor triumphantly writing down the recipe once she and Joe had declared this combination the best. Sonja wasn't sure, but she thought Joe was reliving that day as well.

"What does it mean?" Sonja hoped he knew. She hoped he would share.

Joe pulled the manual back up to his face. "Three cups of Columbian roast for every one cup of French Columbian roast," Joe grinned. "But here's the real secret. Three pinches of salt if you're making the large pot full up, and one pinch of salt if you're making the half-size one. That's all there is to it."

"Salt? Really?" Sonja questioned.

"Yep. Salt. But," Joe lowered his voice to a whisper, "I wouldn't go around shoutin' it out to everybody. Gotta have some trade secrets, right?"

"Right," Sonja smiled. She decided not to tell him she was on her way to a trade show, where professionals would pass on their own trade secrets. Secrets she trusted more than the memory of this old man. However, when she looked at the writing on the cover, Joe's explanation made sense. It may be worth a try.

Sonja picked up one of the Western novels Joe set on the table beside him. "I don't have long, but would you like me to read some to you?" she offered.

"That would be good. But not one of those. I'm in the middle of another good book." Joe pushed his wheelchair over to his bedside table and returned with a large book on his lap. Sonja recognized it immediately. A knot formed in her throat.

CHAPTER 7

"OVERWHELMING." IT WAS THE ONLY word Sonja could think of to describe the Coffee Brewers Trade Show and Symposium. "I spent most of the day in the exhibitor's hall walking up and down long aisles of vendor booths. They had everything from coffee equipment and supplies to furniture, bakery needs, and rows upon rows of coffee suppliers."

Daniel Parker picked up one of the many brochures Sonja had strewn across the dining room table. "What exactly are you hoping to get out of this?" her father asked.

"I just need to learn the business. I think I need to know what's out there." Sonja pulled her business plan from her laptop case and handed it to her father for his inspection. "I wrote it up, even though I know I don't have investors or anything. I remember how you used to tell me to always set goals for the long term and smaller ones along the way. That's what I did. That way I'll be able to track my progress, Daddy."

Daniel Parker shuffled the papers in his hand. "Things have sure changed. When I started my landscaping business, I didn't write a mission and vision statement. My mission was to work hard, and my vision was to make a living. But I'm proud of you, Sonja. I'll read every word. So, if you ladies will excuse me . . . "

"Your grandmother would be very happy to see how you are investing the money she left you," Annette told her daughter as Daniel sequestered himself in the living room to read Sonja's plan.

"I would rather have Grandma Grace here than her money."

"Me, too. But still, you make us all proud. I'm glad you had a good day."

"Mom, you wouldn't believe that place. They have chocolate-covered everything, and I'm pretty sure I've sampled enough coffee to keep me awake for a week." Sonja plopped down on the couch. "And this is only the opening day! The workshops start tomorrow. Right now, I feel like vegging out."

"I like your plan," Daniel said as he joined them twenty minutes later. "But like I said before, I think you'd be smart to keep everything status quo this first year of operation."

"Maybe. Though I keep thinking I want something to put my mark on the store."

"Like what?"

"Eventually, I'd like an espresso machine. But at least it'd be great to offer some sort of specialty flavor or cookie or something. That's why I wanted Mom's recipe for breakfast cookies."

"I'll back you on your mother's cookies; but when it comes to all those special coffees, you might consider getting to know your clientele first. I think back to when I first started the garden center . . . " As her father talked, Sonja's caffeine intake proved less than she estimated. An hour later, her mother woke her, suggesting she go to bed. Six in the morning would come all too quickly.

* * *

The hall housing the workshop called "Barista for Beginners: For Those Who Don't Know 'Beans' About Coffee" was standing room only. Obviously, she was not the only rookie attending the show. A tall, dark-haired woman sitting about three rows from the back waved to her. There was an empty seat next to her. The woman signaled Sonja to come sit. Sonja hesitated; but after looking around the room, she realized it was probably the only vacant chair available.

"Thanks." She sat down and put her bag filled with pamphlets and samples under her chair.

"No, thank you," the woman whispered. "See the big redhead in the back?"

Sonja glanced over her shoulder. A very large, redheaded woman was standing near the door. Sonja had seen her earlier at one of the chocolate booths.

"Uh-huh." Did this woman not want the redhead to sit beside her because of her size? If so, she thought she just might excuse herself and offer the chair to Ms. Redheaded Lady.

"She wanted to sit here, but her perfume was so strong, I couldn't breathe. I lied and told her I was holding the chair for a friend. My name is Cindy. What's yours, friend?"

Sonja couldn't help but laugh. "Sonja."

Cindy and Sonja sat through the lecture. The audio system wasn't the best for a room this size. When it came to the question and answer time, they could hear only the answer. The speaker didn't repeat the question for everyone, and he only called on people in the first few rows. Finally, the two decided to find the food court for lunch.

Cindy sat at a high-top and unloaded her tray of food. "I worked in a coffee shop during college; so, after graduation, I landed a job managing a café in Chicago. Alec, my boss, sent me here to see what trends are coming up next."

"So, what were you doing in basic coffee 101?" Sonja asked.

"Like the workshop title says, I don't know beans about coffee. I'm a good manager, and I know how to hire and fire. I also know to let my experienced baristas train my newbies. I figure it's time I learn more about what I'm doing."

"But you said you worked in a coffee shop in college."

"Scrubbing tables and washing dishes."

"So, did you learn anything today?"

"Not really. You?" Cindy asked.

"Some." As the two women ate, Sonja told Cindy about Libby's Cuppa Joe.

"That's a bold step," Cindy told her. "I wish I had the courage to do something like that." The two exchanged email addresses and spent the rest of the afternoon wandering through the exhibitor hall together.

"Any advice?" Sonja asked.

"All I can say is that the espresso machine is the heart of a good coffee shop."

"The only thing is, I don't have twelve thousand dollars to spend on an espresso machine. I looked at every model here, I think, and pelted every vendor with questions, but . . . " Maybe her dad was right. Stick to the status quo for now.

"Hey, you don't have to do everything your first year. From what you've told me, it sounds like the previous owners did what they did well. That's good business, right?"

"I think you're right. I need to just learn to do my best with what I have now; and maybe next year, I can think about adding on."

Making that decision narrowed Sonja's workshop options for the next three days. She decided to not attend the symposium on espresso and eliminated the workshop on global markets. She did go to the one about Fair Trade Coffees and one on the following day about using social media to market your café.

"I'm not coming back tomorrow," Cindy told her as they ate their slices of Chicago pizza the next to last day. "It's only a half day, and I'm really tired."

"I know what you mean. Every night, I drive two hours to get back to my parents' house; and I'm so wound up, I sit on my bed half the night and go through all of the materials I picked up that day. I'm exhausted."

Sonja drove back to Kenosha after lunch. She had seen enough. Heard enough. Sampled enough. But she had learned a lot. The representative from the same company who manufactured her double air pot brewing system was most helpful. He taught her how to use and clean the machine.

No espresso machine. No new coffees or ideas I can use this year. Now what? Guess it's back to status quo.

CHAPTER 8

"YOU'RE HOME EARLY," DANIEL CALLED out to Sonja when he arrived home from work.

Annette was close behind. "You cooked dinner? I could get used to this. Come home from work to a homemade meal."

"Nearly homemade," Sonja confessed. "I just bought one of those hot roasted chickens at the grocery, then made the rest here."

"I smell sautéed onions and garlic. And is that summer squash and zucchini?" Annette peeked into the large wok skillet.

"Yep. And then I added tomatoes. I cooked up a box of penne pasta. It's my version of pasta primavera. I love it with roasted chicken."

Daniel Parker raved over his daughter's cooking skills. Annette said she hadn't eaten anything so delicious.

"Well, in truth, I have only about three meals. But this *is* one of my favorites." The three spent the evening on the patio by the fire pit. Sonja pulled an old, tattered quilt around her and shared what she had learned at the trade show the last few days. "I decided to let some of what I learned sink in, so I'm taking the last day off. It's only a half-day anyway."

"Does that mean another home-cooked meal?" Daniel licked his lips.

"On Friday? On pizza night? Never! But I'll pick up the pizza, if you like."

The next morning brought with it the luxury of sleeping in late. By the time she crept down the stairs, both of the older Parkers had already left for work. Sonja poured herself a cup of coffee, warmed it in the microwave, and helped herself to a bowl of cereal and a not-so-ripe banana. She sat down at the kitchen table to plan her day. The free day was a gift. It meant she wouldn't have to wait to shop for the painting supplies she needed for Libby's. As she ate her cold breakfast, she looked over the list of supplies as well as the items she wanted to recover from the trunks she still had stored in her parents' basement.

Today was Annette's last day of teaching before spring break. Her offer to spend the following week helping Sonja paint the coffee shop was perfect. *Perfect for me, anyway.* Daniel would be on his own for the week but would come to Door County on Easter's eve. The thought crossed Sonja's mind that if she got everything ready today, she could talk her mother into leaving a day early. She really didn't want to go to church, yet knew it would be expected.

Sonja checked the time on her cell phone. "Let's see, Central time here, Pacific time there. Perfect." She'd catch Fran before she left for the office.

"Sonja! I wondered when I'd hear from you. Got your email. I can't figure out the time thing, so I hesitated calling. Sounds like you've been busy." Fran never changed. She chatted away nonstop for the next few minutes, filling Sonja in on the latest office news. "So how is it being back with your parents? Feeling the 'mother smother' yet?"

Fran had a knack for shooting an arrow straight into the one thing you didn't want to share but knew you needed to talk about.

"My mom isn't like that exactly. Okay, maybe a little, but . . ."

"But what?"

"I'm in Kenosha for the weekend; and I know they'll expect me to go to church with them Sunday, and I really don't want to go. I think I kind of left church in college. And you know I never went when I lived in California."

"Yeah, but you talked about people you knew and stuff you did as if you liked all that church stuff."

"I grew up in the Westside First Community Church, and yeah, it was okay. I mean, some of it was great. Like youth group and Vacation Bible School."

"So, you have friends there, right?"

"Sort of. I mean, I do. But—" How could she explain? Gina and Liz were both married with kids. They had been childhood friends, but she had outgrown them. And there would be people asking when she was going to settle down and get married.

Most would not understand her desire to run her own business. Some would suggest she go into business with her father if she wanted to work. Gina would be okay, perhaps even interested in her new venture with the coffee shop. But Liz would have the name of a "really super guy" for her. Sonja knew how the day would run. It was the same every time she visited home. Every time she attended church with her parents. Even though she didn't want to go, she knew she would. Her parents counted on it.

"Most of those people knew me as a child."

"I think I understand," Fran said. "It's the old saying, 'You can never go back.' Just take it for what it is. I say, have fun, then hit the road for Fish Bait."

The corners of Sonja's mouth curled up. "Fish Creek."

"Whatever. You rock, and that's all that matters. Hey, I gotta get out of here, or I'll be late for work."

I rock. Sonja dressed quickly and headed to the home improvement store. For the dining area, she chose a soft gray for three of the walls and a brick red for the fourth. She picked out paint for the living quarters as well. Sonja chose three brushes, paint rollers, a roller pan, filler to prep the walls, some sandpaper, and blue tape. She found a small toolbox with an assortment of tools in it. *Yep, I rock. Watch out Fish Creek; here I come.*

Sonja looked at the time on her cell phone as she stood in line to check out of the store. It was still before noon. A quick call to Parker's Lawn and Landscaping confirmed her dad was on a job in northern Illinois. She got the address from Lila, her father's office assistant, picked up his favorite chicken sandwich from a local restaurant, and surprised him at the multimillion dollar estate he was transforming for the Easter holiday.

"Hey there!" Daniel jumped off the bed of the truck. "How's my little girl?" The two sat on the side of the flatbed truck that once held the bags of mulch his crew was now distributing around the trees and newly planted shrubs.

"You're such an artist, Dad," Sonja told her father as she looked around the grounds surrounding the large house.

"The key is to make it look natural, as if God put it there."

Sonja had heard this philosophy before. When a customer wanted a waterfall in the backyard, Daniel would talk to them about how it needed to look as though it belonged there. He had a knack for taking a small space and making it look big and a large space feel intimate.

"I picked out a sort of earthy, light, limestone gray color for my walls," she said.

"I thought maybe you would pick out 'coffee' or 'mocha.'" Daniel bit into his sandwich.

"That would have been great, but they didn't have those colors. I don't have many choices with the coffee either." Sonja went on to describe the West Coast coffee shops she had enjoyed in California. "Someday, I want to bring a bit of California to Door County. Hopefully, I'll make enough money this year to buy an espresso machine."

"What happened to keeping it status quo?" Daniel asked.

"Status quo is fine for the first year, Dad; but let's face it—just serving plain old coffee day in and day out is boring."

"I can see that." Daniel rubbed his chin. "If all I did was dig in the dirt day in and day out, I would get bored, too."

Sonja looked at her father. She knew that look. He was quiet, giving her time to think. He had some point to make. She didn't want to hear it.

"It's different for you, Daddy. You do something different for every client. You give them what they want."

"Exactly. And maybe all your customers want is a good cup of coffee, a welcoming place to sit and relax, maybe read a book or play a game. Maybe they'll just sit on the porch and munch on a cookie. You're giving them something they're looking for when they come to Door County. Peace. Quiet. Relaxation. Maybe they're looking for Door County, not California."

"I could live with that perspective for a while." It might help. Status quo should at least pay the bills. She didn't want to admit to her father the weariness washing over her as she lay awake at night wondering if she had made the right decision.

CHAPTER 9

SONJA WAS TOTALLY CAUGHT OFF-GUARD when, during the hard-fought Monopoly game on Friday night, her mother suggested they leave on Saturday instead of Sunday.

"You have everything we need, and it'll give us an extra day to paint."

"I guess I figured you'd not want to leave until after church," Sonja said.

"We'll go to your church."

"Sure. Uh, I haven't really claimed a church yet. I know the Linders asked if I wanted to go to church with them, but it's in Sister Bay."

"Is that far?"

"I guess not."

Annette Parker was almost as passionate about painting as she was about teaching. As soon as they arrived on Saturday, she set to work. She showed Sonja how to fill in the holes and blemishes in the walls. They waited until the compound dried, then sanded down the area until it was smooth. They worked well into the late evening hours and even spent a few hours Sunday evening sanding and priming what would become the accent wall with a pink primer.

"Tell me this will not stay like this," Sonja moaned. "It looks like someone threw up in here."

Annette laughed. "Just the primer you need for an even covering of the red, sweetie. I promise."

Monday morning, the two prepped the main dining area of the coffee shop to paint. Filling in the small pockmarks was fun. Taping around all of the woodwork and windows was tedious. The ceiling was made of painted tin, square tiles. Even though it was chipped and peeled in places, Sonja liked the effect. She did not want to paint the ceiling. Applying the blue tape to the tin tiles where the ceiling met the top of the walls was the most difficult. The stepladder that came with the place was too short for the high ceiling. Sonja had to borrow a taller one from Craig Linder.

"The Linders seem like nice people," Annette remarked as the two once again moved the ladder to a new position.

"Uh-huh."

The whole Linder family was the first to greet Sonja and Annette the day before at church. "I really liked the sermon yesterday, too. Didn't you?"

"Uh-huh." Sonja pretended to be engrossed in a particularly difficult part of getting the tape on the ceiling tile just right. "This doesn't want to lay flat," she complained.

Sonja could hardly remember a sermon she barely heard. She had been busy creating yet another "To Do" list in her head. Whenever others around her made a sermon note on their church bulletin, Sonja took the opportunity to jot down her latest idea for the shop.

"Most of the time, the sermon on Palm Sunday is all about Jesus riding into Jerusalem and everybody celebrating," Annette continued. "But learning about the significance of the Passover . . . Wasn't that interesting?"

I should have paid more attention. Something about the lamb. Sonja searched her mind for fragments of the morning message. But once everything was taped, the painting consumed the next several days.

Tuesday, Wednesday, and Thursday were three long days of painting. Sonja was grateful for her mother's help. Annette was tireless. Driven. Up early, to bed late, Annette accomplished more in her week at Libby's than Sonja had done since she arrived.

"We might as well clean all these lights, while we have the ladder," she would say. Or, "I'll make you some new curtains for this window. What did you have in mind?"

The two women took few breaks but managed a long walk after dinner each evening. Sonja introduced her to the neighbors she had met. She shared what she knew about the woman who lived in the cottage next to the pottery house.

"Joan told me her name is Margaret Atchinson. We've never met, but sometimes I can feel her eyes watching me."

Annette cast a wary look over her shoulder as they crossed the road. "That's kind of eerie."

"It's not scary. From what Joan said, I think she and Libby were longtime friends. Maybe it's just hard for her."

Annette put her arm around her daughter. "You've always looked for the good in people, haven't you? I am so proud of you, Sonja Parker!"

Rose, from the library, came by Thursday afternoon to help paint. Cassie Linder pitched in as well, and Joan Linder made a pot of chili for the whole crew. By early Friday, the painting was complete.

Daniel Parker would be up Saturday around dinnertime, so the Parker women wanted everything to look its best when he arrived. Having stowed the last of the paint cans and drop cloths, Sonja and her mother stood in the dining room doorway and admired their work. The red wall had required the most repair and the odd pink primer, but the end result was exactly what Sonja had envisioned. The lace curtains draping the front windows had been removed. Sonja liked the mix of the old tin ceiling and woodwork of the Victorian building with the crisp, modern colors. She decided to add Roman shades on the front windows instead of the lace curtains. If she couldn't find what she wanted, Annette promised to make them for her.

Friday afternoon was spent baking breakfast cookies. Annette was thrilled to use the giant standing mixer with its dough hooks.

"This is a really stiff dough," Annette explained. "I usually have to just get in there with my hands and mix it up."

"I'm pretty sure the Board of Health would be happy to know you have discovered dough hooks, Mom." Warmth spread through Sonja. It had been a good week.

One thing Sonja did not want to do was to put up the old framed prints of farms and fishing boats she had inherited with the coffee shop. Since arriving, she shot pictures of the Fish Creek area. Now enlarged and printed in black and white, Sonja laid the photos out on the tables in the dining area. It was another way of mixing the old with the new. While the first batch of cookies baked, Annette looked over the array of pictures Sonja had taken and helped her pick out six of the best shots.

"You should have been a photographer," Annette told her daughter. "You have your father's eye for beauty."

By the time Daniel Parker arrived on Saturday evening, the transformation of the main floor of the coffee shop was complete. He walked through the rooms in silence. "It doesn't even look like the same place. I mean it's so fresh and new-looking. I like it!"

After dinner Sonja showed her parents the electric, metal contraption she and Cassie found in the cabinet and the beautiful tea set from "Occupied Japan."

"Well, I don't know what that metal thing is," Annette began, "but this tea set is exquisite, and I expect it's pretty valuable. A lot of people collect china made in occupied Japan. Have you checked it out?"

"I looked online," Sonja said. "I found the pattern, but I didn't find any complete sets like this. Where do I go from here?"

Daniel picked up the metal piece. "There's a man in Waukegan who collects that stuff. I did his landscaping for him. But I'm wondering just what this thing does." He turned the metal contraption over in his hands. "Aha! I think I know what this is. I think it's an antique toaster."

"Do you think you could take this stuff home and maybe even find a buyer? I really don't know where to begin." Sonja packed the found treasures in one of her many empty boxes. It was late. Sister Bay Community Church was offering a sunrise service for Easter Sunday. The three agreed that if they were able to get up that early, they would make a sincere effort to attend the special service.

"So, tell me about your church," Daniel inquired of his daughter. It was time to pull out the reasons Sonja had offered her mother as to why she hadn't been going to church here. It didn't matter that she didn't attend church in California. She had managed to go to enough concerts or special events and report on those. The one time her parents had visited over a Sunday, Sonja planned a visit up the coast for them.

"I don't know much about the church, actually," Sonja began. "When I first got here, I took forever to adjust to the time change. It would be seven in the morning, and I should be getting up, but it felt like five a.m. The Linders invited me, but I didn't have a chance to check it out until last Sunday. But it was pretty good, right, Mom?"

The tactic worked. Annette started talking about the sermon. Sonja intended to read the passages listed in the sermon notes. She could use the excuse she was busy, but in truth, she wasn't sure where her Bible was located. *Probably in one of the boxes I brought up last weekend.* Sonja listened as her mother talked enthusiastically about how the minister had explained the symbolism of the Passover lamb.

"The pastor explained how the Israelites, serving as slaves in Egypt, were told to sacrifice a perfect lamb and paint the blood of the lamb over their doors. The Angel of Death would be passing through that night and taking the lives of the firstborn throughout Egypt," Annette began. "He told how God promised that the Angel of Death would see the blood, recognize a sacrifice had already been made for that household, and 'pass over' that family. I've heard the story a million times, but then he likened Jesus to the Passover lamb, pure and perfect, a sacrifice made so that we would have eternal life. The sacrifice had already been made.

"And the way he told it, well, it just made it all come alive, you know," Annette concluded.

Sonja listened with as much interest as her father. *How could the story have escaped me?*

Sunday morning, Sonja's parents were up and ready when she reluctantly crawled out of bed. She had given the full bed to her parents and slept on the twin bed in the second bedroom. She awoke to the sounds of her parents talking in the kitchen. Getting ready as quickly as possible, Sonja gulped a quick cup of coffee and indulged in two of the breakfast cookies before heading out the door for the much-anticipated sunrise service. It turned out to be both simple and beautiful. Sonja enjoyed the service more than she expected.

Daniel helped out on Monday with a couple of minor repairs. He fixed a latch on a cabinet door that wouldn't quite catch and fixed the screen on the back door. Then he carefully surveyed the yard surrounding the coffee shop, pulling an errant weed here and there and making notes about the landscaping. As he worked, Sonja and her mother washed the rest of the windows.

By the time the older Parkers left, Sonja was ready for a nap. She had what her mother called "a good kind of tired." She had thirty-one dozen cookies in her big freezer in the coffee shop. Her dining room was painted, polished, and ready for customers, and even her downstairs apartment had a new look. The light fixtures throughout the building had been cleaned; and new, brighter bulbs replaced old, dim ones. Sonja's bedroom walls bore a muted shade of green called "restful." Now, Sonja decided to test the wall color out. It was dark when she awoke from her nap. She decided "restful" was appropriately named.

Her parents would be back in three weeks for her "soft opening." She had her work cut out for her if everything was going to be ready.

CHAPTER 10

"I LOVE THE COLOR."

"The coffee is good."

"Does it look bigger to you?"

For the most part, the comments Sonja heard at the "soft opening" she held for the locals were positive. The turnout was fairly large. With Joan's help, Sonja had sent out forty invitations to the year-round residents of Fish Creek. She sent invitations to all of the other businesses and posted a note in what the locals referred to as "The Weekly," a local newspaper serving all of Door County.

Designing the invitations proved more difficult than expected. The first drafts said something about the coffee shop being "under new management." Sonja decided it sounded as if something was wrong with the old management. It was offensive, and she knew it.

She tried "keeping the tradition" or "in honor of Libby and Joe Davis," but neither were true. She was trying to expand, to break tradition; and although she had gained great respect for the two people who started the business, she wanted the night to be an introduction of the new look of Libby's Cuppa Joe and of her as the new owner. Finally, Sonja found the right words.

You are cordially invited

to an

Open House Gathering

Libby's Cuppa Joe

Sunday, April 25

1:00 p.m.-4:00 p.m.

151 Main Street

Fish Creek, WI

New Look, Same Coffee

Sonja Parker, Proprietor

Sonja was happy she had taken Joe at his word about the coffee recipe. When she tried it, she knew why everyone she met claimed Libby's had the best coffee on the peninsula. She didn't need all of the fancy beans and grinders and costly coffees she had seen at the trade show. She just needed the recipe, coffee delivered from her supplier in Green Bay, a little salt, and her mother to guide her as to what constituted "a pinch."

Annette and Daniel arrived early to help their daughter with the event. Cassie kept the coffee and cookies flowing. At first, Sonja greeted each guest at the door; but then Daniel took over, so Sonja could talk with everyone. She tried to remember names and connect people to their businesses. At one point, she looked up to see Rose walking around with a tray of cookies. Sonja carefully tracked the creamers used, any flavors requested, how much real sugar was used and how much artificial. She was counting on data from the soft opening to guide her in planning for her real opening, just a couple of weeks away.

No one needed to tell her the biscotti she had ordered especially for the event was not up to the standards to which the locals held Libby's. Remnants of the long Italian biscuits folded in napkins and left on the pretty paper plates rested on tables around the room. Her guests also passed over the expensive, intricately decorated specialty cookies, choosing, instead, the lumpy, thawed-out breakfast cookies her mother had made.

Several people had asked what kind of cookies they were, raving about how great they were with coffee. Many wanted to know if she was a relative of Libby and Joe. Most were pleased to learn she had visited Joe, and all wanted a report on how he was faring in his retirement.

Something inside told Sonja she needed to protect Joe. To make sure the picture she painted was accurate but not one that made people pity him.

"Oh, he was in great spirits; and I don't know how old the man is, but boy is he sharp!" Everyone nodded and smiled.

"Sounds like Joe," an older gentleman said.

"I heard he moved to a retirement village," someone said. "Sounds nice."

Sonja thought of the place Joe now called home. What were the positives she could share?

"He seems to like it, too," she responded. "They have a place bigger than this dining room where people get together to play games and such."

Someone chuckled. "That's Joe for you. He always loved a good game of chess or checkers."

"Remember the time that man from Chicago came, and they got into a chess game that lasted all night?" another local recalled. Soon people were sharing memories of both Libby and Joe. Fond memories.

"I have to admit, honey, I think you're going to do great with this little shop," Annette told her daughter that evening. "I was hesitant. I mean, the restaurant business is tough. Your dad has always been the one with the entrepreneurial spirit."

"You have no idea what that means to me, Mom."

The next two weeks Sonja spent baking three versions of the breakfast cookies. She made eight dozen of the traditional recipe and another eight dozen with almonds in them. She tried eight dozen more with raisins and eight dozen with butterscotch chips. She hoped they would all "freeze nicely."

She searched the internet for easy recipes to make muffins. One all-bran muffin recipe looked delicious but was only good served fresh out of the oven. Joan gave her a cherry chip muffin recipe, promising it would be a big hit. It would have to be, Sonja thought to herself. It was both complicated and costly. Finally, she stocked up on boxed muffin mixes and called it quits.

What she had in the freezer—the remaining biscotti and special-order cookies, along with the muffin mixes—would have to see her through the first month of operation. Sonja had visions of the hundreds of visitors coming to Door County for vacation seeking out her store, coming back for more, and sending all their friends.

She was wrong. Although there were a few "early birds," as Joan Linder called them, in May, the first real wave of vacationers came on the scene after Memorial Day. For the first month of business, the locals remained Sonja's best customers. When the ranger from Peninsula State Park stopped by for lunch, Sonja served him a peanut butter and jelly sandwich with three breakfast cookies. On the house. He was a nice man. He had one cup of coffee with his sandwich and took another with him. Sonja was happy school wasn't out until June. She couldn't afford to pay Cassie until business picked up.

When a farmer stopped by for lunch and asked about the meat choice, Sonja fed him a peanut butter and jelly sandwich as well. On the house. The house couldn't keep providing free lunches. Fortunately, in addition to making a great veggie and spaghetti casserole, Sonja knew how to make chicken salad. She did so every morning from that day on, offering her guests either a peanut butter and jelly sandwich or a meat choice.

By mid-June, Sonja had Cassie working full-time. Vacationers made up most of the customer list, though a few locals still stopped in from time to time. Late in July, a man dressed in overalls with a plain white t-shirt underneath came walking in around ten in the morning. He was young and rather good-looking in a scruffy sort of way. Sonja immediately pegged him as a local. He was dressed like one of the dairy farmers who often stopped by when they came to town. Dairy farmers were up early. *But lunch at ten? Not unlikely.* Instead, the man ordered a coffee and one of the muffins Sonja had made from a mix. It wasn't bad, just a little dry. Made drier by sitting out on a tray all morning.

The man was talking on his cell phone. He took a bite of the dry muffin, made a face, put it down, drained his cup of coffee, and left.

I should have given it to him free. Still, he was a bit rude. He didn't say anything except to order his coffee and point to the muffins. Most locals at least say hello. Or how about please or thank you? She would have settled for an "I can't eat this." Instead, he simply stood and walked out, leaving the remnant of the dry muffin on the table, crumbs everywhere. "Good riddance," Sonja muttered under her breath.

Business was steady but not exactly booming. Comparing her financial records for the summer months against the three years before Libby got sick helped Sonja realize she wasn't a total failure. Yet. She only needed to make it through the next couple of months. According to locals, everything would slow down a bit in late August and September but would surge again with the pumpkin festival in October. *Then I'll close shop, regroup, and come back next year, armed with a better understanding of what I need to do to make this business flourish.*

It was the first Tuesday in September. A slow day by any measure. Sonja was in the midst of chopping pimentos when her cell phone rang.

"Hello! It's Cindy!" *Cindy?* Ah, yes, the woman whose company she enjoyed at the trade show. The two had stayed in touch through emails, but this phone call was the first time Sonja had heard her new friend's voice in months. "Cindy Owens, from the trade show," the voice confirmed, as if reading Sonja's mind.

"Of course! It took me a minute. Sorry," Sonja admitted. "How are you?"

"Terrific. Listen, remember when I emailed you and told you I may get a position with a new store?"

"Did you get it?"

"I did! It's in Steamboat Springs, Colorado!"

"That's fantastic! You're so lucky!" Sonja loved Colorado. She had been there several times on ski trips during her college years.

"I *am* lucky, and so are you," Cindy said. "That is, if you still have the dream of spending your off-season someplace totally incredible."

"I don't understand." Sonja leaned against the counter and held her breath.

"I am the new manager of the Rocky Mountain Coffee Bar in Steamboat. I need a somewhat-experienced but eager-to-learn-more assistant. I decided to hire you! What are you doing right now?"

"I'm learning how to make pimento cheese," Sonja replied, looking at the pile of cheese, mayonnaise, and chopped pimento in her bowl.

"Can't you just buy that in little tubs at the grocery?"

"Yeah, well . . . " Sonja didn't have time to explain how she learned the hard way that you get more for your money when you make it yourself. Cindy was already pressing on.

"I want you to get on your computer and go to this website." Sonja wrote down the web address. "Oh, and then be sure to check your emails. I sent you a job description and application. Gotta keep this on the up-and-up," Cindy continued.

Sonja's heart raced. She washed her hands and opened the computer. The job description and application form popped up. Cindy was looking for a senior barista to assist her in overseeing all baristas, as well as control the inventory, order supplies, and make sure the store was in compliance with all health standards.

Sonja called her back. "As much as I hate to say this, I'm not qualified. I've had no real experience as a barista."

"Not to worry. I've learned a lot, and I'll personally train you in everything you need to know."

Once Sonja accepted the position, she found herself thinking about the prospects all the time. Under Cindy's tutelage, Sonja knew she would be able to make Libby's a real coffee shop. *A free education. No, better than that. I'll be getting paid to get an education.*

Sonja found it hard to concentrate on anything for the next few weeks. She made lists of what clothes she needed to pack and what ski equipment she would take. Cindy offered her a room in her condo. It may not be ideal to room with your boss, but it was certainly more economical.

The only glitch to the trip came when Sonja told her parents about her plans.

"You'll be there for Christmas?" Annette asked.

"I know you kind of wanted to do something here. Don't you see? This is my chance to learn the business firsthand. And I'll be able to make some money."

Annette looked down at her hands and bit her lip.

"I haven't been home for Christmas for the past three Christmases, anyway. I didn't think . . . "

"But we came to California that first year, and I figured since you were so close now . . . "

"Come on, girls," Daniel said. "It's one day. We get to see Sonja much more now throughout the year, and that's what matters, right?"

Annette looked up and patted Sonja's hand. "Sorry, Sonja. I guess I'm being a little selfish. I wasn't thinking. You said you wanted to have a winter job when the shop was closed. This is a great opportunity for you, honey."

Sonja and Cindy were talking daily now. When she mentioned how her parents were feeling, Cindy offered the perfect solution.

"Look, the franchise is putting me up in this three-bedroom condo. Invite your parents for Christmas. They'll love it, and I'll be spending the Christmas weekend in Dillon, anyway."

I can do better than merely invite them. If I dip into my emergency fund, I can fly them out to Steamboat for Christmas. A perfect Christmas gift. All I'll have to do is replace the cost of tickets with money I earn in Steamboat. I love my life! All that is left is to make it through the pumpkin festival, pack up, and go. What could go wrong?

CHAPTER 11

EGG HARBOR'S PUMPKIN FESTIVAL TRAFFIC put Libby's in the black. Barely. If she had had a stiff mortgage payment to pay, she could have declared bankruptcy. Sonja whispered a thank you under her breath to Grandma Grace, who left her enough money to buy the business and have enough cushion to get it running. Sonja's business plan allowed for three years to begin making money. She hoped in five years to show a clear and growing profit. All she had to do was hold her own the first two or three years. By the middle of October, Sonja had packed her things in her red Corolla and was heading down the highway. One stop in Green Bay, and then a week in Kenosha, where she would leave her car at her parent's house and fly to her new adventure.

Joe was in good spirits when she arrived at Happy Years.

"How's Libby's doin' for you? Tell me all about the pumpkin festival . . . What's that you got there?"

Sonja filled him in on the success of the pumpkin festival as she opened the package of sugar-free cookies she had picked up at the market in Egg Harbor. "And Libby's is doing great."

"Service with a smile," he told her. "Remember that. It's the key to success." It was cliché, but she took it to heart.

"I thought you might like these." Sonja opened a grocery bag revealing several copies of the Door County weekly, *The Advocate*. The old newspapers had been a last-minute thought. She almost didn't pack them, due to Joe's poor eyesight; but when she pulled out the newspapers, Sonja knew she could have given him nothing better.

"Shall I read you the headlines?"

"No, no. I want to hear the obits."

Sonja crinkled her nose. "Uh, okay." She turned to the obituaries and began reading.

"Now, that fellow was a good man," Joe would say. Or, "I remember him. He was younger than me!" He didn't seem to be particularly sad or upset. Curious. *That's it—curious.* Not morbid or depressed. Simply curious.

Once she read the obituaries in several issues, Joe asked her to read a few short articles and announcements of upcoming events.

Sonja looked sideways at the wristwatch Joe wore. "I'm afraid I have to leave now, Joe." *Should I tell him I've closed the shop for the winter? No.* "I won't be back for a while."

"I understand, Judy." Joe rubbed the back of his hand across his eye. *Did he call me Judy? Was he crying?*

Sonja stopped at the desk on the way out. "Mr. Davis seemed so sad today when I left."

"Oh, they all get like that."

"He called me Judy."

"I think that's his daughter. Mr. Joe talks about her some. I think she must come on weekends 'cause I never met her yet."

* * *

Now, three weeks later, Sonja looked around the busy coffee bar in Steamboat. People of all ages were clustered at tables, talking about the upcoming winter season and the winter festival. She wondered if

Joe ever got out to the gathering room at Happy Years. He was a man who had enjoyed the company of others every day all year long.

Libby's may not be the same. *But if it is a place where friends can meet and enjoy each other's company, perhaps Joe's legacy will live on.* Sonja smiled. *Along with new specialty coffees.*

Cindy was right. In no time, Sonja was creating lattes, cappuccinos, espressos, and macchiatos and serving a variety of each, adding flavorings, creams, caramel, and whipped cream on top. Making the coffees proved easy. She needed only to follow each recipe carefully. It was a matter of measuring, timing, and sequencing. And smiling.

Cindy's condominium was spacious and accommodating for both of them. The three-bedroom, two-bath apartment looked out over the Yampa river.

"The early trappers and settlers in Colorado's Rocky Mountains thought the bubbling hot water springs feeding the Yampa sounded like a steamboat churning its way up the winding river. That's how Steamboat got its name," Cindy explained.

The mountains surrounding the Western town drew ski enthusiasts by day, and the warm springs lured aching bodies and partygoers by night.

A bus stop outside the building was a direct line to the town, with all its shops and history, or it could be taken the opposite direction to the base of the ski mountain. When the weather was sunny, Sonja walked through the parking lot to the back of the property and walked the paved pathway from the condo complex into town and her new job.

With training and work, Sonja had little time to ski until the week after Thanksgiving, when business at the coffee shop slowed enough to warrant a day off mid-week. She went skiing a few times with one of the baristas Cindy had hired from town. By the third week of December, though, tourist business was booming again.

Christmas week turned out to be the busiest week of the season. Families flocked to the resort area every year during the holidays. This year, however, was particularly crowded. Christmas fell on a Saturday. Most of the rental condo units were booked for Saturday arrival and Saturday departure.

Sonja's parents arrived on the Friday before Christmas with a schedule to leave on a Sunday, the day after New Year's Day. Their stay was stretched a bit longer than Sonja originally planned. She told them they could stay for the week. Of course, she didn't expect them to take her up on it. Not traveling on the actual holidays, though, would make their travel experience less hectic. Unfortunately, Cindy's plan to be in Dillon for the weekend meant Sonja was in charge of the store on Sunday, the day after Christmas. Cindy originally wanted the shop open on Christmas day. The staff grumbled. After discussing it with Sonja, Cindy gave in and opened only for the afternoon when the onslaught of guests would be arriving.

Sunday and Monday evenings were always busy. Vacationers had settled in and were anxious to now explore the Western town. This Sunday, the day after Christmas, was the busiest day Sonja had experienced since arriving in Steamboat. One of the baristas scheduled for the morning did not show up, meaning Sonja and a young, newly trained man named Joel had to take care of the morning crowd. The second shift of workers arrived around one. Sonja left Carrie, the most experienced of the three, in charge, while she had dinner with her parents and took a short nap. She returned to the store at seven to help with the evening crowd and closing.

"If I'd had any idea how crazy the day after Christmas would be, I would have returned earlier," Cindy assured Sonja. "Take Monday off. But do me a favor and check in around lunch, just in case."

Sonja called from the top of the ski slope shortly after noon to see that all was well at the store. She and her father were about to tackle their first black diamond run of the day. Annette had begged off, skiing down an easier trail and promising to meet them at the lodge for lunch.

"The crowd is manageable now, but could you come in after dinner to help close up?"

Sonja slowly shook her head and pressed her lips together. *Hadn't she already put in her time?* The day before had been exhausting. She blew out her breath. "I can be there by seven."

"Make it six," Cindy said and abruptly hung up. Sonja was regretting the call. A couple more runs on the slopes, a quick change of clothes back at the condo, and Sonja managed to show up at the shop a few minutes before six. Though she was tired, she delivered service with a smile, as Joe had advised.

"That's the closest I've come to wishing I hadn't taken the job." Sonja sat on the edge of the bed in her parents' room as they packed to leave.

Annette folded a sweater and put it in her now-full suitcase. "You seem to be enjoying the work."

"I am. I mean I'm really learning the business. I kind of have a vision for Libby's that looks a lot like the Rocky Mountain Coffee Bar. I've taken more notes here than I did as a freshman in college English and doing more research to boot."

Annette sat down beside Sonja and stroked her daughter's hair. "We're very proud of you, Sonja. Thanks for such a wonderful week."

Sonja leaned in and hugged her mother. "I'm just glad you and Daddy came."

"One of the benefits of being a teacher, I guess."

Daniel emerged from the living room. "And having a successful daughter."

Sonja beamed. Her parents didn't need to know she still had a long way to go to replace the fifteen hundred dollars it cost for their airfare and still save enough for a down payment on a top-of-the-line espresso machine.

"I have to admit, I wasn't all that sure about you coming out here." Daniel waved his hand in the air. "I know. I know. I talk a good game, but like your mom, I kind of wanted you to stick around Wisconsin for the holidays, too. But I have to say, I think this has been great for you. It's the perfect time in your life to do it. One day, you'll be married and all, and then you won't be able to just pick up and go off for a winter like this."

Sonja smiled at her father. "Exactly. Who knows what next year will bring?"

Sonja was having fun. She met other townies working the winter in Steamboat just so they could ski. There was never a shortage of friends to ski with on her days off or to go out with in the evenings when she wasn't working and wasn't too tired.

Cindy was not an avid skier. She was, however, an avid partygoer. The best parties were after hours on Wednesday or Thursday nights. The workload for those days was typically lighter, and the young crowd that constituted ninety percent of the workforce could afford to party into the night and sleep in a little later the next morning. It was at one of these late-night gatherings toward the end of February when Sonja met Damon.

CHAPTER 12

DAMON EVANS WORKED AS A part-time ski instructor. "But my real passion is to be a writer." He described to Sonja in detail the storyline of his latest novel.

"My agent says it will be epic," Damon boasted. "I actually think there will be a movie deal out of it."

Sonja was impressed. "A movie?"

"My agent is working on a contract with a major publishing house and the movie rights simultaneously."

"Who's publishing it?"

Damon leaned in conspiratorially. "I'm not allowed to say anything until everything on both sides is signed, sealed, and delivered." He offered a mischievous smile. "But trust me, you'll be the first to know."

Damon had traveled the world. His stories of hiking the bush country of Australia and taking a boat down the Amazon made him one of the most interesting people Sonja had ever known. The thirty-two-year-old man had attended three prestigious universities. "I always knew I wanted to write a book, so eventually, I had to walk away from the stale, conformist views of those professors.

"The only way to write about life is to experience it," he told Sonja.

It didn't hurt that Damon was tall and good-looking. He had dark brown eyes with long lashes that would have been the envy of most women. His hair was black and curly to the point of being unruly. He was a popular ski instructor. Especially among the wealthy women in their fifties, looking to improve their downhill form. Yet, from all Sonja could discern, Damon remained unaffected by the attention of his clientele.

Damon Evans soon became a regular at the Rocky Mountain Coffee Bar.

"He may bring his notebook and pen with him and drink several cups of coffee," Joel noted, "but something tells me he's more interested in a certain assistant manager than his writing or the coffee."

Damon arranged his schedule to match Sonja's so that the two of them could ski together.

"I don't trust that man," Cindy told Sonja one morning. "You be careful. Don't lose your heart to him."

"I like him. He's interesting."

"Tell him you love him, and he'll hit the road in the blink of an eye," Cindy warned. "His type wants one thing and one thing only."

"He's not like that," Sonja argued. "He has never so much as made a pass at me and kissed me only once. And that was on the cheek." Cindy's warning stung. Damon was one of the good guys. Couldn't Cindy see that? *And I'm careful to guard both my words and my heart. Mostly.*

"The truth is," Sonja told her friend Fran in San Diego one evening on the phone, "I think Damon may be the one."

"I've heard that before. Remember Greg?"

"That was a moment—a fling—and you know it. This is real. This is the man I could see myself with for the rest of my life."

Sonja lay across her bed and closed her eyes. *Damon. My Daniel. My Joe.* She didn't mention to Cindy or Fran about Damon's invitation to take her on a late-night excursion to one of the popular hot springs, where after ten o'clock in the evening, bathing suits were optional. After all, she had declined, and he had planned a sleigh ride instead. She came close to revealing her heart to him that night but managed to say nothing. It was already March. She would be leaving in two weeks to return to Door County. She needed to remain focused.

Sonja told Damon all about Libby's Cuppa Joe. At first, he laughed at the name of both the store and the town where it was located. When she frowned, he quickly apologized. Damon had never been to Wisconsin.

"Door County is beautiful. You should come see Libby's for yourself. I know you'd like it."

"Maybe. Sometime." Damon covered her hand with his.

"Anytime." Sonja hoped she sounded light. "You might even find something there you could use in your book. Like, maybe instead of having the terrorists attack New York City, they could attack Chicago. Then they could hide in a cabin in Door County!" Sonja's imagination was running now.

Damon laughed. "You're a funny one. Always coming up with ideas."

"I can see it. Lake Michigan. The boats."

Damon pushed a lock of her hair from her forehead. "And a pretty girl who happens to live in a coffee shop?"

Sonja's skin grew warm. She turned away. "Maybe." *A young woman the hero would love and protect.*

Damon stood. "I do need to get back to the book. I've been neglecting it for . . . " He leaned in so his forehead was touching hers. " . . . other interests."

Sonja raised her head and looked into Damon's dark brown eyes. "Will you be back later?"

He kissed her cheek and stood to leave. "Later."

The next two weeks flew by. As soon as the college spring break sessions ended, the skiing crowd waned.

Sonja brought a large latte to Damon's table. "What will you do now? I mean the ski season is slowing down. It has to be tough without clients."

"All the rich people will be heading to the beaches for spring break. I have a buddy in West Palm."

"Florida?" Sonja's heart sank.

"Don't look so glum. How about a special dinner tonight on the mountain?"

Sonja tilted her head and looked into Damon's grinning face. "How could I say no?"

A few hours later, Damon gently tucked a soft velvet throw over her as they boarded the gondola to ascend the mountain. The view at night was spectacular. Lights throughout the Yampa Valley looked like diamonds glistening in the snow.

"I don't think I've ever known anyone like you," Damon cooed in Sonja's ear. "I'd rather be here with you than anywhere else on the face of the earth."

The mountain restaurant lit with white fairy lights appeared past the tall evergreens. The evening air was cool and clear.

"Their roasted chicken is the best," Damon told her.

They placed their order and sat holding hands. Damon moved the candle from the center of the table. "That's better. I want to see your whole face."

I could live like this forever. Sonja shivered.

"Are you cold?" Damon asked.

"No. Just realizing I have only a few more days until I fly back to the real world. I hate the idea of leaving Neverland." The weak laugh she offered did little to convince either of them she wasn't sad at the prospect.

On the way down from the magical evening, Damon put his arm around her and pulled her close, kissing her gently on the lips. Sonja wanted to hear words of love and commitment, but they never came.

Damon held her close. His hands stroked her back. His hold was powerful, and he began kissing her hard. Just then, the gondola's cable passed roughly over one of the pulleys on the pole above. Sonja pressed her hands against Damon's chest and pushed him away.

"I . . . I . . . can't," she managed to say. Cindy's warning haunted her.

Damon looked in her face. "You know I care."

"I do, but . . . "

"But what?"

"Not now. Not yet."

Damon eased back, a hurt look on his face. Sonja couldn't explain. She wanted him to hold her. She longed for his kiss; but more than that, Sonja needed his love. His respect. They rode the gondola the rest of the way down in silence.

Damon softened a bit on the ride home. He reached his hand over to hold hers. Sonja felt her heart melting. A love song Sonja recognized as an oldie her parents often listened to filled the car. Damon adjusted the fan blowing warm air into the small space, moving it down a notch. He turned and smiled at Sonja.

When Damon dropped her off, he wanted to come in. She considered it. It was late. He pulled her close.

"It is late. But I don't have to go home. And I'll be quiet. Susan won't even know I'm here."

Sonja frowned as she pushed him away. "I . . . I can't. I hope you understand."

"But Sonja, I care about you." Damon stroked her cheek, gently moving an errant strand of her hair back behind her ear.

Sonja looked up. "We would regret it in the morning."

"I wouldn't."

"But I would. I value our relationship too much to give in to a night of passion."

Damon turned and left, leaving Sonja to fumble to open the door for herself. Once inside, she breathed deeply as she leaned against the closed door. Sonja waited until she heard the engine of his car come to life before wandering to her room. Greg, the man she had dated in California, had suggested nearly the same thing. But Greg was easy to turn down. Her resolve with Damon was weaker. *What if there's another time?* The sleepless night came with Sonja reliving the evening. Her thoughts waivered between "I did what was right," and "I'm an adult. I should be able to do what I want."

The next morning, a message was waiting for her at the coffee bar. Damon had left. Sonja cried off and on for three days. Then on the fourth, she received a text. *Got a gig in Florida. Sorry I had to leave without saying goodbye. Will call as soon as I get settled. Love, Damon.*

Sonja read the message over and over. *Love, Damon. He said he cared. He used the word "love."* Sonja was glad she had held her ground that last night.

But now, everything was different. Sonja turned her attention to her last days in Steamboat and her plans for her own little store in Door County.

"Remember, you can come back next year," Cindy assured her as the two said their goodbyes at the small local airport.

Sonja stood on the tarmac and looked toward the mountain. Their mountain. Everything was perfect. Life was good. Nothing could take this away from her. Nothing.

CHAPTER 13

SONJA REVIEWED HER "TO DO" list during her two-hour layover at the Denver airport. She hadn't socked away the twelve thousand dollars she needed to buy the espresso machine of her dreams, but she had a plan. She could buy the machine on credit with a small down payment. Sonja did the math.

"The income it produces will be more than enough to replace the money in my emergency fund and still make the payments."

"Were you talking to me, miss?"

Sonja looked up from her hard, plastic chair in the waiting area. An older man stared at her. "No. Sorry. I guess I was talking to myself."

"No apology necessary. I do it all the time."

Sonja set up her laptop and logged in on the airport's WiFi. She studied the picture of the espresso machine she had selected. The company's representative assured her she could order the unit online, and it would be delivered in three to five business days. *If I order it the day I get back to the shop, I'll have plenty of time to get it up and running for the season.*

Friday night meant pizza night for the Parkers in Kenosha, where Sonja had left her car for the winter. The three Parkers sat around the table and fell naturally into the rhythm and dialogue that made their family close.

Annette offered her daughter another piece of pizza. "You're not staying? I hoped you'd spend a few days with us."

"I know. But I have a little less than a month to get everything ready to open. I want to practice using the new espresso machine and do some promo work to get the word out that Libby's Cuppa Joe has entered the twenty-first century. Uh, maybe not that way."

"Yeah, not sure I'd put it that way," Daniel said. "Someone is bound to be offended."

"Right. I'll have to think about that. I do intend to create an advertising blitz for the whole county, though."

"Are you going to stop and see Joe?"

"I don't think so, Mom. I might get everything ready and then take a day to drive back to Green Bay before the season starts."

"He's a good man," Annette said. "I'm glad you're staying in touch."

The April sunshine promised a good beginning for the second season. Her anticipation heightened as the little red car, laden with groceries and a box of books her mother had collected for the coffee shop's bookshelves, crawled up the highway. This year, she was prepared. Sonja touched the notebook with her "To Do" list.

No painting. No going through the cabinets. A sense of peace washed over her. *Okay, maybe this year, I'll tackle the large attic storage room with its sloping ceilings and mountains of boxes.* "Who knows? Maybe I'll even find some more treasures."

The metal contraption she and Cassie found in the kitchen turned out to be an antique toaster, as her dad predicted. Annette sold it online for $105.00. Her dad had taken the tea set made in occupied Japan to his client in Waukegan, who offered Sonja two hundred dollars for it. She said she would think about it. Somehow, Sonja had the feeling the beautiful china set was worth more. Now, as she drove, she was thinking about putting money from the sale of the toaster and whatever she could get for the tea set toward her coveted espresso machine.

Sonja made the turn onto Main Street in Fish Creek. A smile covered her face. Home. The sun was low in the western sky. A soft glow of orange engulfed her Victorian dwelling. Sonja was anxious to get into the building but took a moment to appreciate the beauty of the sunset. Finally, gathering two bags of the groceries, Sonja made her way to the back door of the lower level, the door to the living quarters of Libby's Cuppa Joe.

An odd, earthy smell hit her hard. She made a face. Sonja stepped over the threshold and heard the squish of water, even as her shoes sank into the wet carpet.

"What?" Sonja asked aloud. She squished her way across the living room floor and put the grocery bags on her kitchen table. She had turned the water off before she left for the winter. *Where did this come from?* Sonja looked at her watch. Her first inclination was to call home. She valued her dad's knowledge of such matters. Her father had put in a full day. He would be tired. This was his busy season. *This is it. Time to grow up. Time to act like a real business woman.* Sonja tried to think. She called the Linder household. In ten minutes, Craig Linder was standing in her apartment, a flashlight and tools in hand.

"Did you turn off your water? Did you drain your lines?" Craig went through a list of questions. He finally asked her to show him exactly what she did. She showed him that each valve under each sink was turned off. He went into the cellar area of the basement level where the main waterline came into the building. He investigated everything.

"You didn't turn off the main waterline," he explained.

"I thought the turn off was under each sink. I closed each of those and then just turned all the faucets on to drain them," Sonja admitted.

"Well, you needed to turn off the mainline coming into the house, turn all the faucets on, and drain the toilets dry. Some people even put that pink antifreeze stuff you get for campers in their drains and traps when they leave for the winter. And you should have turned the outside faucet on as well. It's the lowest water outlet and would have helped drain the lines."

Sonja was on the verge of tears. She pulled her mouth tight. She thought she understood what she needed to do to prepare her house for the cold Wisconsin winter.

"I kept the heat set at fifty-five. That's what the Elstons from the glass shop told me to do. Now what?"

Craig Linder rubbed the back of his neck. "You'll need a plumber and probably a contractor. But don't worry. Stuff like this happens all the time. Probably a power outage let it get too cold. We have them sometimes. You'll be okay. It'll just be a little out of pocket, that's all. I'll see about getting some friends from church tomorrow to help me pull up the carpet. Maybe we'll get a better idea of where the leak is tomorrow."

"Should I call the plumber tonight?"

Craig scratched his head. "The thing is, the damage has been done. We have the water off now; and if you call someone now, you'll have to pay the weekend emergency rates. But if you'd feel better about it . . . "

"No, that's okay. I'll call Monday."

"You can't stay here. Joan said to bring you to our house. You'll have to share with Cassie, but at least you'll have a bathroom. Bring your groceries. We'll find room for them." Craig picked up the grocery bag nearest him and headed for the door.

Joan Linder must've been watching for them when Sonja and Craig came up the stairs to the apartment above the bait and tackle store. She welcomed Sonja with a hug and a large bowl of homemade chili. Sonja sank into the kitchen chair and allowed her friend to put the perishable groceries from her purchases away, while she indulged in the hot, spicy chili. She listened as Craig told his wife how a pipe had burst. Sonja was grateful he didn't make it sound as if she was a fool.

"You know, it could have been worse," Joan said. "One year, the photographer's studio flooded, and the plumber estimated enough water had pumped into that place to fill a swimming pool. He lost every bit of his equipment."

"Don't forget the Conaways, you know, from church," Craig added. "They had a summer home that flooded one winter. By the time they returned, mold started to grow."

Sonja knew they were telling her she was in better shape than others, but the message she took to bed with her that night was that the mess may be worse than she expected. Cassie gave up her bed to Sonja, opting instead to sleep on the couch. As Sonja lay awake in bed worrying about the state of her coffee shop, she looked at the teen posters and paper flowers hanging on the wall. A small bulletin board above Cassie's desk was filled with pictures of Cassie and her friends. *If only my problems were those of a teen. What to wear, where to go on Saturday night, or finishing a group project on time seemed like major decisions when I was Cassie's age.*

What sleep she did get was fitful. Images of mold growing up through the walls of Libby's plagued her with each passing minute.

The Linders were up and ready for church when Sonja made her way to the small kitchen. "I don't think I'll be going to church this morning," Sonja told her friends over breakfast.

Joan patted Sonja's hand. "Did you get any sleep at all last night?"

"Not much. I need to get over to Libby's and check everything. You understand, don't you?"

"Of course, we do."

"And I'll see about getting some help from some of our church friends," Craig said. "Don't worry, Sonja. Everything will right itself. May be a little out of pocket, that's all. You'll see."

Sonja trudged to the coffee shop. There it was again. *A little out of pocket. I wish I knew what he thinks constitutes a little out of pocket.*

Once Sonja was certain the damage was limited to her basement living quarters, she breathed a sigh of relief. She could, in theory, move a bed up into the large open room on the upper floor if significant repairs had to be made. She unloaded her backpack from her car. *What else should I take inside?* The books could wait. She'd take her car back to the Linders', so she'd have clothes for the next few days.

What if there is mold? Mold could be the end of Libby's Cuppa Joe in Fish Creek.

Sonja looked at her phone. It was too early to call her parents. They would be at church. Instead, she sat on the stairs leading up to the coffee shop kitchen and drafted a text to Damon. It was hard to describe all that she was facing without sounding whiney or as if she was making a big thing out of nothing. She finally erased most of what she drafted and simply sent the message, "Call me. Emergency."

While she waited for a response, she decided to pick everything up off her bedroom closet floors and pack her pictures, books, and knickknacks lying about so if furniture needed to be moved, nothing would be in the way. She waited all of an hour and then decided to try to call Damon's cell phone again. "I got home and discovered my pipes were broken at the store. I don't know what to do," she cried into Damon's voicemail.

Now, all she could do was wait. Sonja looked at her watch. Her parents would be out of church by now. She hesitated. It would be good to solve this problem on her own, yet she was smart enough to know they offered a perspective she should consider. After she had practiced what she called her "voice of confidence," she dialed her mother's cell phone.

Annette Parker turned on the speaker function of her cell phone when she heard Sonja begin to describe finding water in her living quarters and Craig Linder's assessment of broken pipes. Sonja managed to keep her voice even and her mood light, assuring them she had everything under control.

"Craig Linder recommended a plumber. I'm calling him tomorrow morning. I'll let you know what he says."

"Have you called your insurance company yet?" Daniel asked his daughter

"Your homeowner's policy should cover the costs. There may be a deductible or something, though. Let us know if you need us to help."

"You've already helped a ton, Dad. I didn't even think about insurance covering the damage!" Sonja responded. "Even the Linders didn't think of it. Some people from their church are coming over today to help with cleanup."

Sonja ended the call with a renewed hope. She knew her homeowner's policy covered things like theft or damage from a fire. If they would cover the water damage, her money worries would be over. *The Linders probably didn't mention it because it was so obvious. They probably thought I would think of that one myself.* She had just looked up the contact information for her insurance claims department when the entire Linder family, along with a half-dozen other friends from church, showed up at her door ready to help her clean up the mess downstairs.

The church group pulled up the carpet, rolling it up and taking the soaking wet mass to the dumpster near the end of Main Street. At her request, they moved the twin bed to the upper room, so Sonja could move back into her own home once the plumbing problem was addressed. Joan, Sonja, Cassie, and a woman named Linda scoured the entire concrete floor with disinfectant. Now if the insurance company would come through, everything would be back on track.

CHAPTER 14

SONJA SPENT MOST OF MONDAY morning cleaning everything the water had damaged. At first, she thought the problem was limited to the living room area. Later, she found water pooled under the refrigerator and stove in the kitchen. The lower cabinets also had water damage, and the lower part of the wall between the kitchen and bathroom was cold, wet, and soft to the touch. Sonja sat down on the steps leading upstairs and cried.

I wish I could just close the door to the entire lower level and pretend it didn't exist.

Walter Freedman, the plumber Craig Linder recommended, promised to be at the coffee shop sometime between noon and four Monday afternoon. Her insurance company told her an insurance adjustor named Ms. Stanton would be by to assess the situation before five Monday evening. Sonja paced the floor, looking out the window every time she heard a car rolling down the street.

Ms. Stanton arrived around one o'clock. She smiled and handed Sonja her card. She was all business. Sonja took her down the stairs.

"I would offer you a cup of coffee, but the water is off," Sonja said with what she hoped was a sweet smile. "Actually, this is the worst thing I think I've ever experienced."

Ms. Stanton had little to say. She walked around, took notes, and asked Sonja to recount the mishap.

"Well, I came home Saturday. I had been away for the winter. I noticed the floor was wet first. And then I called my neighbor. He's the one who turned the water off," Sonja offered. "And then some people from church came over yesterday to help with the cleanup. They're the ones who pulled up all of the wet, smelly carpet for me, and we got most of the water mopped up."

Ms. Stanton was writing it all down. "You went away for the whole winter and hadn't turned the water off?"

"I thought I did." She explained how she thought the turn off was the valve located under each sink.

Ms. Stanton listened to the explanation and wrote what Sonja said down on her notepad. "Did the plumber give you an estimate of the cost and time frame to fix it?"

"Oh, he hasn't been here yet. I called him this morning, and he's going to come this afternoon."

Ms. Stanton narrowed her eyes, her glare shooting arrows at Sonja as if she had committed the most heinous of crimes. "You didn't call him until this morning?"

Sonja didn't know how to read this woman. She mumbled something about it being the weekend and tried to explain that she had done everything she could to clean the mess up. Ms. Stanton walked through the apartment opening doors to closets and cabinets. She asked to see the rest of the building.

Finally, Ms. Stanton closed her notebook and clicked her pen shut. "I'll file my report by the end of the week. A claims agent will process it. Send a copy of the plumber's estimate as soon as you get it as well as the estimate for new carpeting and any construction work." The woman almost smiled as she left. Almost.

Ms. Stanton had been businesslike and, at times, abrupt; but as she walked down the front steps, Sonja was hopeful her insurance policy would pay off. She was just about to call her parents with a report of the visit when Walter Freedman's truck pulled in the driveway.

"Just call me Walter," he said, extending a rough hand. Walter was a wiry man with a black beard and wide smile. Sonja had the impression he would have made a great pirate. She escorted him to the lower level, then returned to the upstairs dining area where she called Craig, who offered to be her second pair of ears when it came to dealing with the repairmen she would need. Having someone who understood the plumbing lingo nearby when Walter explained what needed to be done would be a boon.

By the time Craig showed up on her doorstep, Walter was emerging from the depths of Libby's Cuppa Joe. The news wasn't good. Craig had the name of a good local contractor. A phone call later, and Libby's was crawling with repairmen.

Walter finally called it a day. As he loaded the last of his tools in his truck, Sonja took a deep breath. *I need someone to talk to. Should I call my parents?* She dialed Fran's number in San Diego. "Fran?" But it was Fran's voicemail doing all the talking.

Twenty minutes later, Sonja dredged up the courage to call her parents. "They don't need to know everything," Sonja told herself. "I need not tell them of my diminishing cash reserve."

Sonja closed her eyes. *Everything's under control. Everything's under control. Everything's under control.* Sonja stood and moved to the front window of the shop as she dialed her dad's cell number.

"Do you need me to drive up?" Daniel Parker asked.

"Not yet. Maybe Easter? Like last year?" Sonja suggested. "That's when I could really use some help. Easter is late this year, and the Linders think we'll have a lot of people here for spring break, since it should be warmer."

"So, you just think of us as cheap labor?" joked Daniel.

"No, Daddy, not cheap. Free." It felt good to laugh. "Seriously, I have a great plumber; a contractor who is giving me a good price on fixing my wall; and my friend Rose is going carpet shopping with me this weekend."

"Did this contractor you hired look into possible mold or mildew problems?"

"Yes, he did, Dad. He's doing a complete cleanup for me and at a terrific price. He knew Libby and Joe Davis and said that they would have wanted him to help me."

It was a stretch. What Al, the contractor, actually said was something about how he would do it because he would hate for Joe Davis to hear what a mess the new owner had made of the place. Of course, he didn't say that to Sonja directly. She overheard him talking to Walter. She didn't care as long as the building was repaired and mold-free in time for the season of summer tourists.

The process was long. Like dominoes lined up in a perfect order. Walter had to finish the plumbing, so Al from AE Contractors could send in his crew to treat the walls and make the needed repairs. Once that was done, the carpet could be installed and the apartment repainted. Sonja wasn't happy about repainting the apartment. She liked the green she had chosen the first time. She searched but couldn't find it in any of the Door County Stores.

"You could do one thing for me, Dad."

"Name it."

"I liked that green called Restful I used for the walls in the apartment but can't find it here. Do you think you could grab a gallon? Al's treating the walls, so I think I'll need to do some repainting."

"Consider it done. I'm just glad there's something I can do, honey. We'll be up Easter weekend in our paint clothes."

Walter took three days to complete his repairs. There were two small splits in two separate pipes. The pipes had to be replaced. To do so meant changing some other fittings as well. Sonja wrote the check.

Al delivered two large dehumidifiers to draw the moisture out of the air. He then came with three helpers the day after Walter left and began the task of "shooting" chemicals to kill mold into the walls. He removed all of the baseboards in the basement living quarters, cleaning behind them and replacing a few. He tore down the water-soaked wall between the bathroom and kitchen and rebuilt it. To complete the wall, he said some electrical wires should be moved. "An electrician should be called to deal with that." Sonja wrote two more checks.

On Saturday, Sonja and Rose drove to a carpet store in Sturgeon Bay with the measurements in hand. After an hour of looking, Sonja settled for a carpet that was affordable and durable. It wasn't beautiful, but the color was neutral; and since it was a stock item, the company representative promised he could have it delivered and installed in two weeks' time, the timeline the contractor had given her for the completion of his part of the job. Sonja wrote another check.

The now financially strapped owner of Libby's once again contacted her insurance company, having allowed the full "seven to ten business days" promised. The claims department representative pulled up her file on the computer. "Yes, Ms. Parker. I see here it's being processed."

At least with the water turned on, Sonja could live in her own home. The Linders had been generous in allowing her to spend the three nights with them until Walter declared the plumbing sound. She could now use the coffee shop kitchen and the shop's single bathroom. She was glad she had asked the men from the Linder's church to move the twin bed up to the upper floor. She could sleep under her own roof.

Sleep didn't come easy the first night. The room was large and cavernous. The window was uncovered. The house creaked and groaned through the night. And she was cold. Twice she had to trek downstairs to find an extra blanket. *This is temporary.* By the time the season started, she would be back in her own bed. One advantage of spending so much time in the upper room turned out to be the many ideas Sonja came up with for using the space.

There was no door at the top of the stairs, so the vast space was really a part of the coffee shop. One idea was to rent the space out for small parties or to maybe host special teas by reservation only. Sonja toyed with the idea of starting a book club in the space. She considered inviting local authors in to read or have book signings. That would bring traffic into Libby's.

Perhaps when Damon's book is published, he'll come. Total engagement in his writing was the only reason Sonja could accept for not hearing from him. *He cares. He loves me. He'll come.* She imagined him there with her. She allowed herself to daydream about a future with him by her side. Sonja looked around the room. *Perhaps this will be his writing loft.*

Al and his men were still working downstairs. Sonja made a batch of breakfast cookies and a carafe of coffee. She took two dozen of the tasty treats down to the three men, along with a pot full of freshly brewed coffee. Even if they had not wanted to stop the work for a snack, the smell of the fresh coffee and warm cookies lured them to the table.

"Well, I have to tell you one thing, missy. Your coffee is as good as Libby's; I'll give you that."

"Thank you. Joe gave me the secret recipe."

Al put his cookie down. "Is that a fact? When did he do that?"

He thinks I'm lying. "Last season. He's a great guy."

"How do you know Joe?"

"I visited him in Green Bay." Sonja took in a deep breath, put her shoulders back, and stood tall. She could see the man's attitude about his work change with the smile he offered her.

"You're gonna be alright here," he told her. "Better than ever." His crew, which she later learned were really three of his five sons, devoured the cookies hungrily, thanking her for the snack.

Sonja arranged six warm cookies on a paper plate. She pulled on her windbreaker and walked across the lawn of her own property, crossed the road, and right up to the front door of the Atchinson house. She knocked loudly. A rustling from within and the scraping of wood assured her the woman was home. For a split second, the curtains covering the front window moved. Sonja had never met the woman but knew she had been a long-time friend of the Davises.

"Mrs. Atchinson!" Sonja called loudly. "I'm Sonja! I brought you some cookies!" There was no response. "I'll leave them here on the porch!"

A small, inexpensive, wrought iron bistro table with two small chairs sat on the porch beside the front door. Sonja doubted the set was ever used. She set the plate of cookies on the table and turned to leave. She had made it down the walkway and almost to the road when she heard the door creak open behind her.

Margaret Atchinson appeared in the open doorway. She stepped out, looked at Sonja, and reached for the cookies.

"That Walter," she said in a hoarse voice, waving her arm toward the coffee shop, "that Walter is a good man." She turned abruptly and went back into her house leaving a dazed Sonja to walk back home.

Walter had finished his work almost a week ago. *Was the old woman confused? Maybe she was waiting to tell me she approved of Walter. Who knows?* Whatever prompted the comment, Sonja hugged herself with the knowledge she had actually made contact with the woman. "Only doing what Libby would have done." Sonja hummed to herself.

The day was looking up. Sonja all but skipped back to her establishment and set about making more cookies to put in the freezer for her opening during the last week of April. If the insurance money arrived within the week, she would still have time to order the espresso maker and offer Door County a new coffee experience. *Then life will be perfect.*

CHAPTER 15

MONDAY. TIME FOR THE FIRST of her twice-a-week calls to her insurance company.

"For claims, hit one . . . "

Sonja didn't listen to the rest of the menu. She had it memorized. She smashed the number four on her phone. She wanted to speak with a representative.

"This is Sue. How may I help you?"

Sonja explained. Again. "I'm sorry to seem like such a nuisance. It's just that I am running a business here, and I need to get the money from my claim."

The woman on the other end of the line sounded sympathetic; but when she checked the claim number, she had no new information to share. "I can put you through to the manager's voicemail . . . "

Sonja sighed. "No, that's okay. I've left several messages already. Isn't there someone else I can talk to?"

"I can put a flag on your file."

"Uh-huh." The picture of a file folder painted as the American flag blowing in the breeze popped in her mind. *Probably won't be settled until the Fourth of July.* She sighed as she ended the call and set about making plans for rest of the week. Plans that didn't involve an espresso machine.

During the first season, Sonja introduced a few coffee-flavored syrups. Now that she knew more about the industry and how to mix flavors, she ordered four new syrups. Most were available online, but the brand of caramel apple flavoring combination she wanted was not. The company had a wholesaler in Green Bay. The representative volunteered to come to her shop, which was probably the wiser choice, but she wanted to do some other shopping as well. And she needed to see Joe.

She called Joan. "Hey, I was wondering if you might be up to enjoy a 'girls' day out' tomorrow. I know it's late notice, but I need to go to Green Bay to pick up some things, and I thought we could stop by and see Joe."

"Are you kidding? I'd love it! I'd welcome the change in scenery. What time?"

"I'm thinking we can leave early in the morning, say, six or six-thirty? Or later, if you like. We'll grab breakfast out and then go see Joe."

"Six-thirty sounds great. Craig can get the kids off to school. What time should I tell him we'll be back?"

"In time for dinner, I guess."

Sonja spent the rest of Monday afternoon making diabetic cookies to take to Joe. Just before they were to leave, Sonja made a short pot of coffee using Libby's recipe. She poured it into two thermos bottles and picked up her passenger.

"I say we have breakfast in Sturgeon Bay. Maybe something quick. We can enjoy a leisurely lunch and do our shopping after we see Joe. How does that sound?"

"Sounds fine to me," Joan agreed. "I'm just along for the ride."

She may have been just along for the ride, but Sonja couldn't help noticing Joan was wearing makeup and earrings. The navy blue slacks and light blue crew neck sweater looked good with Joan's dark hair.

"This is fun," Joan said as they left Sturgeon Bay. "I rarely eat breakfast out."

The two chatted like old friends as they traveled toward Green Bay.

"Craig said the repairs are going nicely."

"Al didn't seem to think much of me when he started, but I think I'm winning him over."

"I'm sure he just doesn't like change. He and Joe were pretty good friends. But you're a sweet girl. He'll get to know you."

"I'm not sure it's my sweetness that won him over. I think it's the cookies."

Drawing closer to Happy Years Retirement Village, Sonja squirmed. "I think I should warn you about something. Uh . . . despite its name, uh . . . Happy Years Retirement Village is not a village. And it isn't exactly a particularly happy place."

"I know. Craig tracked Joe down at Christmastime. It was decent of you to protect him. That's what you were doing when you made the place sound so nice, right?"

"I just didn't want people to pity him. I don't think he would like that."

Happy Years Retirement Village hadn't changed. *So, Craig Linder had paid a visit.* It was good Joan knew what to expect. The two women wove their way through the maze of hallways and wheelchairs to Joe's room. Although the door was open, Joan knocked lightly. Once again, Joe was sitting in a wheelchair, his back to them. They walked in.

"Joe?" Joan called out. "It's me, Joan Linder."

"Joan! Joan!" Joe called out, turning his chair so that he now faced them. "How good to see you!"

"Sonja drove me," Joan motioned toward the door. "You remember Sonja? She's the woman who bought the coffee shop."

Joe's eyes moved slowly to Sonja. "Of course. Did you try that recipe we discussed?" he asked with a conspiratorial wink.

"I not only tried it. I brought you some." Sonja held up the thermos in her hand. "And . . . I brought you some cookies. Diabetic cookies."

Joan pulled out the cups, napkins, and plates Sonja had packed. Sonja poured the coffee.

"I didn't know how you take your coffee, so I brought a little of everything," she told him.

"Take it in a cup!" Joe jested. He took the hot, black coffee in his hands, brought it to his face, and smelled it. He closed his eyes.

Sonja looked at Joan, then back at Joe. The man kept his eyes closed for a minute more, then pulled the cup back to his lips and took a sip. Sonja waited.

"Tastes like home." Joe reached for a cookie. "You say these are diabetic?"

"Well, yes, sugar-free. I found the best recipe I could on the internet."

"You made 'em?" Joe asked.

"Yes, sir."

Joe took a bite and smiled. "You're gonna do just fine with Libby's."

The three sat and shared their coffee. Joan caught Joe up on all the local news. Sonja listened with interest. She learned more about her neighbors and community over the next half hour than she had in the entire previous season.

"And how's this little girl doing?" Joe asked, giving a nod to Sonja. "She takin' care of Libby's?"

Joan looked at Sonja before she answered. "Sonja is doing great. She's taking excellent care of the place. Baking and keeping it like you and Libby did."

* * *

"Thank you for that," Sonja told her companion as they exited the building a little while later. "Thank you for protecting Joe."

"I did it for you, too, you know," Joan answered. "We all like you and think you're doing fine."

"I feel like a fool. I was so full of myself, I didn't ask for help, just figured I knew what I was doing and nearly turned Libby's into the local swimming hole!"

"But you handled it. And you learned. Sometimes, that's the best you can do."

The day in Green Bay was successful, but moreover, it was fun. Sonja had connected to the people of her new home. Joe was the past. Joan opened the door to the present. Libby's Cuppa Joe was her future.

Everything was going to work out. She would prove she could handle this bump in the road on her own. The insurance check would come, larger-than-ever crowds of people would come to Door County this year, and she would set a new record for sales at Libby's Cuppa Joe.

If only Damon would call.

CHAPTER 16

DANIEL AND ANNETTE PARKER ARRIVED earlier than expected the day before Easter, having left the final landscaping job in the capable hands of a longtime employee. Daniel was anxious to survey the damaged living quarters and pleased with the now-completed work. Annette told her daughter the carpet looked lovely. Sonja had to admit, everything was beginning to take shape. The three Parkers set about painting immediately until the little bell above the front door rang, announcing a customer.

Though Libby's wasn't officially open, the locals had already started coming in early for coffee and a muffin or for a sandwich at lunchtime. Sonja had warmed to the idea of providing homemade baked goods for her community. It turned out her best customers were local patrons who enjoyed meeting each other at the coffee shop each morning to start their day. The lunch crowd varied. All were receptive to whatever "meat choice" Sonja offered each day in addition to the ever-present peanut butter and jelly sandwich.

As eggs had been on sale for the past week in honor of Easter, Sonja offered either fried egg sandwiches or egg salad sandwiches for a couple of days. She thought no one would want the egg offerings for at least a week after Easter, so she offered them before the crowd tired of eating hard boiled eggs left over from the holiday.

Three men, all dressed in work clothes, were waiting at the counter when Sonja emerged from her painting job downstairs. Two of the men ordered egg salad sandwiches, but the third asked if she had any fresh muffins. Sonja recognized the man. He was the same scruffy-looking farmer who had been so rude to her last fall.

"All out of muffins," she said coldly. "I have some breakfast cookies, though, if you like."

"Those are really good, Kevin. I had them here before," one of the other men said. "In fact, I'll take some of those, too."

The man called Kevin ordered cookies as well with his coffee, then, almost as an afterthought, decided to order an egg salad sandwich as well. Sonja gave them their coffees and watched as the three sat down at a table near the front window. She quickly made the sandwiches and filled a plate with cookies. As she placed the order on the table in front of the men, the one called Kevin looked up, smiled, and thanked her. *Maybe he was just having a bad day that day.* She looked back to the table when she reached the kitchen door. What were the men doing? They weren't eating. Had she forgotten something? No, wait. They were praying.

Other shopkeepers and a couple of women from the local bank drifted in for lunch as well. The Linder boys came with Joan. Rose dropped by around two o'clock. She had to settle for peanut butter and jelly, since the egg salad was long gone. Rose stayed and helped finish the day's painting, then accepted Sonja's invitation to join them for spaghetti casserole.

Sonja was grateful. She knew a discussion of her finances wouldn't come up with company. Not that her parents would pry. It was more likely that she would be tempted to talk about her plight as the evening wore on. Sonja knew her parents would feel compelled to step in and help. No, Rose was doing her a favor by staying for dinner. Of that, Sonja was sure.

Sunday morning, Sonja was genuinely surprised to receive an Easter basket from her parents: a washtub filled with plants her father had brought from his own shop to landscape Sonja's front yard. He unloaded the tub, watered the plants, and set it at the end of her porch.

The three headed to the sunrise service, then returned home to change their clothes. Sonja wanted to take them on a hike on the other side of the peninsula to a county park called Caves Point. It was adjacent to the Whitefish Dunes State Park, according to her map. She plotted the destination into her GPS. At least the device would get them to the general vicinity.

The sun-filled day lifted Sonja's spirits. Door County offers an interesting mix of geography. The inner part of the peninsula consists mostly of working farms. Dairy cows dotted the pastures as Sonja drove southeast across County Road A to Jacksonport, then took Highway 57 until she reached another county road, winding back toward the Whitefish Dunes State Park. Sonja had ventured there only once before, so she relied on the GPS to take her to the park entrance.

A trail wound its way along the shore of Lake Michigan. At some points on the trail, the three stood on rock outcroppings high above the lapping water below. The view was spectacular. The trail then took them through the woods before once again emerging from the trees to the shoreline. This time, they were able to easily get to the sandy beach. Daniel put his hand in the cold water and shuddered. Annette sat on a large, smooth stone and looked out over the expanse of water.

"You look out there and suddenly feel so small," she commented.

Sonja smiled. Her mother may feel small; but for Sonja, the water and sunshine gave her a feeling of power and significance. The three sat on the rocks in silence, soaking in the sun, the cove protecting them from the cool breeze. Sonja's thoughts turned to her business venture once more.

"You know, Mom, I think everything is back on track." *My money problems will soon be behind me. If only Damon would get my messages and call.*

Daniel Parker had to drive back to Kenosha to attend to his business but made plans to return the following weekend to pick up Annette, whose spring break fell the week after Easter this year. Daniel had worked hard all week prior to coming to Fish Creek, then worked hard all weekend painting and moving Sonja's twin bed back downstairs, as well as landscaping the front flower bed with the plants he had brought. Now, he would return to another hard week of work. Alone.

Any guilt Sonja harbored that her parents would be separated for the week dissipated as she ate one of her mother's blueberry muffins.

"Will these freeze?"

"You can freeze them. Of course, they're always best fresh out of the oven," Annette told her.

Joan's prediction about the influx of spring break tourists proved true. The warm weather and late Easter drew young families to the resort towns of the peninsula. Sonja's mother baked fresh muffins every morning for the week.

Sonja's peanut butter and jelly sandwiches were gaining in popularity. She was now offering two choices. The traditional sandwich was made with creamy peanut butter and grape jelly on store-bought white or wheat bread. She cut the sandwich with a cookie cutter-type sandwich cutter she had purchased on her day trip to Green Bay. The children were delighted with the sandwiches shaped like dinosaurs.

The new adult offering was as big a hit among the patrons frequenting Libby's. Each morning, a local bakery delivered fresh-baked whole grain bread. Sonja's specialty PB & J featured a chunky peanut butter spread generously on the thickly sliced bread. Sonja added chopped apples and grapes and a topping of jelly. The hearty sandwich was a meal in itself, although Sonja always added cookies to the plate.

The "meat choice" had also taken on a new look. Sonja continued to offer chicken salad, egg salad, or homemade pimento cheese, but she now served each on a choice of croissants or the fresh-baked, grainy, whole wheat bread. Every order included two small breakfast cookies on the side.

The breakfast cookies had become her trademark. They were so popular, she sold them by the dozen, packaged in a small, white paper bag with a label on the front she had designed and printed on her computer. The adhesive label gave the name and address of the store, plus her new website address.

The website was intended to announce the espresso and cappuccino offerings at Libby's. She had worked many of her off hours in Colorado on the design, engaging the help of Damon, who had once worked with computers on one of the campuses where he attended classes for a while. Now with the espresso machine on hold, she had to remove that portion of the website.

Sonja was still pleased with the outcome. The website was beautiful and featured a picture of the building. The description invited readers to come, relax, and enjoy a cup of the finest coffee or tea in Door County. She added pictures of a couple sitting on the front porch looking out over the green lawn as they sipped their coffee. There was another photo of a man playing dominoes with a young boy at a table inside. Yet another picture showed a pleasant, young girl offering a plate of cookies to a pair of grateful guests. The Linders, Parkers, and Rose served well as models in the pictures.

Now with a jumpstart on the season, Sonja was confident. She had no espresso machine, no contingency funds, and a limited amount of cash in the bank. But with a good season predicted ahead, Sonja knew everything in her life would improve once the insurance check arrived.

She had little time to think about Damon over the week. By week's end, she and her mother were exhausted. They had a fairly steady stream of customers each day until around two in the afternoon. When the numbers thinned in the afternoon, they had time to clean the dining room and kitchen and get a fresh start on baking for the next day. Sleep came easily.

By the time Annette was leaving to go back to her "real job," she said teaching her second graders would be a welcome rest. She said it jokingly, but Sonja suspected there was a bit of truth in her mother's comment. During the season, Sonja would open the shop at noon on Sundays, but this was early enough to not bother. This Sunday would truly be a day of rest. Monday's business would come quickly.

"I must insist I speak with a supervisor," Sonja spoke authoritatively into the phone. "It has been over a month since Ms. Stanton came to assess my situation. I turned everything in that she asked to see within the first week. I still have had no communication from your office."

"I'll see what I can do," the voice on the other end of the line replied.

Sonja scrunched her cell phone between her ear and shoulder. *I really should get one of those handsfree wireless headphones.* The music the insurance company's phone service played was periodically interrupted by a man's voice suggesting a variety of special policies with what he called the "people's company." *People's company. Yeah, right.* She spooned a row of Double Chocolate Crunch cookies onto one of her cookie sheets lined up on the kitchen work counter. Five cookie sheets later, a man's voice startled her.

"This is John. How can I help you?" John asked in his friendly voice.

Sonja explained her situation for the hundredth time and said all she needed to know was when she could expect to hear from her claim.

"I'm not trying to be troublesome," she explained. "I just need to know how long this will take. I am running a business, and I need to plan."

"Do you have your account number handy?"

Sonja sighed. John the friendly. John the helpful. John the man who should have her information in front of him. She gave him the number she had been assigned.

"Well, Ms. Parker, our records show we mailed your report and check on Friday. You should get it sometime today or tomorrow."

"Finally! Thank you!" She had done it. She had weathered the storm. She shoved the cookies into the oven and set the timer. The mail wouldn't arrive until late afternoon.

She raced downstairs to get the espresso machine information and the company representative's phone number. It was already the middle of May. *If I order it today, I'll have it by the weekend.*

Sonja saw no need to wait. She would put it on her credit card and pay it off by the end of the season. She took the information with her to the kitchen. She started to dial the number when she heard the roar of a motorcycle and saw the spray of gravel in its wake coming her way. She put the phone down and moved out onto the porch. She was trying to think of something to say to the intruder when he stepped off the bike and pulled at his helmet. There was something familiar . . .

"Anywhere around here where I could get a good cup of coffee?" Damon called out.

Sonja flew down the steps. She jumped into Damon's arms, hugging his neck tightly. Damon smiled, spun her around, set her down, and planted a big kiss on her lips.

"I came as soon as I could."

Sonja drew back. "As soon as you could?"

"Your voicemail. You said your water pipes broke. You sounded so upset, I headed straight here."

"I left that message over a month ago," Sonja told him.

Damon had a surprised look on his face. "I just got the message two days ago. I came as soon as I could."

Sonja took in the hurt look in his eyes. Did he feel as though he had let her down? Sonja wasn't sure, but she couldn't overlook the fact that he was here now. He heard the message. He heard her call for help, dropped everything, and came to her. Now Sonja was sure of his feelings. His actions spoke louder than any words.

Damon parked his motorcycle behind the coffee shop near her car and came back to the front, a backpack slung over his shoulder. She looked around before walking back in the front entrance. She was sure Mrs. Atchinson was watching. *Let her. Damon is here. He came to help.*

Smoke and the piercing whistling of the smoke alarm greeted her as she reentered the building. "The cookies!" Sonja turned off the oven and pulled the blackened cookies from the oven. Damon rushed to open a window. He grabbed a dishtowel and waved the smoke away from the alarm until it finally stopped its shrill sound.

"Are these your specialty cookies I heard so much about?" he asked.

Sonja wanted to cry; but when she looked up, she saw he was grinning. "I got a little distracted," she sighed.

It took a few minutes to clean up the mess. Damon helped.

"I was headed to Florida to take a job on a cruise ship. I stopped in Kansas to see an old friend on the way. Say, do you have a fan? It'd help with getting this smoke out."

"On the service porch." Sonja scraped the blackened remains of the cookies from the metal sheet.

Damon plugged the fan in the outlet and aimed it so it would pull the dark cloud toward the back of the building. "So, anyway, I stopped to see this guy; and it turns out, he has cancer. I skipped the job in Florida and stayed to help him with his farm."

Sonja's heart warmed. Damon was a good man. He dropped his own plans to help his friend, and now he was here helping her.

"You should see his farm, Sonja. It's huge. Miles of nothing. I didn't have internet or cell service."

"So that's why . . . "

Damon stood behind her. He put his arms around her waist. "I hope you can forgive me. I came as soon as I got the message."

Sonja turned to face him. "Nothing to forgive."

With the kitchen clean and a new batch of cookies in the oven, the two sat down with two large cups of coffee.

"Did you get more done on your book?"

"It's coming along. Right now, I want to hear about you. Tell me about the coffee shop. I take it you're doing okay now."

"I would say everything is definitely looking up."

Two customers stopped in for cookies and coffee to go. When they left, Sonja took Damon on a quick tour of the shop and the living quarters below.

He stopped and inspected the work the plumber and the contractor had completed. "I would have used brass here instead of copper."

"Is that bad?" Sonja asked looking over his shoulder.

"Not bad. Probably what was on there before. It's just that these won't last as long."

Sonja tried to dismiss her concerns but made a mental note to call Walter and ask about the fittings. The little bell above the door rang. It was late in the afternoon, and the week looked to be somewhat slow. Sonja ran up the stairs to greet her customers. It was an older couple from Chicago. They ordered coffee and some of the pecan and caramel cookies Sonja had on the counter in a domed cake plate. They sat at a table for two by the window. Sonja watched as the older gentleman held the chair for his wife. *That could be us one day.* Sonja drew in a deep breath. Dreams of all that could be filled her mind as she swept the kitchen floor.

CHAPTER 17

SONJA FOUND ACCOMMODATIONS FOR DAMON at an affordable bed and breakfast in Sister Bay.

"Why can't I stay here? I could move that twin bed upstairs."

Sonja stared at the floor and shook her head. "No. No, you can't."

"Sonja, I wasn't suggesting we . . . uh . . . anything."

"I know, but my neighbors would never understand."

"It's none of their business." Damon threw his hands up in surrender. "Okay, look. I don't want to cause you any grief. You know that, right?"

Sonja stared into his eyes. "I know." She tilted her head and gave Damon a playful nudge with her shoulder. "Sister Bay isn't that far away."

On a good day, Sister Bay was only a fifteen-minute drive, but the bed and breakfast was on the other side of the town. The morning fog made for a long, cool ride on Damon's Harley. Even so, Damon showed up at Libby's before dawn the next few days, ready to help Sonja make coffee, bake, serve, and clean up. Sonja decided to close early Tuesday, Wednesday, and Thursday, so the two of them could explore Door County.

On Tuesday, she took him on a tour of the lighthouses. They boarded the passenger ferry to Washington Island and later ate dinner at a small pub in Bailey's Harbor. It was a full day and late in the evening when the two returned to the coffee shop. After a long kiss goodnight, Damon reluctantly boarded his motorcycle and headed back toward Sister Bay.

Sonja watched from the porch until he had driven out of sight. She turned to retrieve the mail from her box. Ads . . . ads . . . an electric bill . . . and . . . what? An envelope marked with her insurance company's return address. She ripped it open. The check was much smaller than she expected. Perhaps they were paying only for the plumbing with this check, and the repairs and carpet would follow later. *Is that how they did it? Process each part of the claim separately?* She had paid each vendor separately. It made sense.

Sonja carefully read the letter and report accompanying the check. Ms. Stanton had been thorough. Thorough and uncompromising.

> The owner had not taken the proper precautions necessary to winterize the building. The establishment sat for two to three days untouched after the leak had been discovered. At the time of this inspection, the owner said a plumber still had not been in to assess the damage. The carpet had been removed, but it was old. No evidence of mold resulting from the water leak. The building is very old, and the furniture is of thrift store quality.

How would she know how old the carpet was? The basement carpet was long gone before Ms. Stanton arrived! The accompanying letter explained that in light of Ms. Stanton's inspection and subsequent report, they would pay only a percentage of the requested monies on the claim. What they deemed appropriate covered barely a third of what Sonja had spent on repairs. She held the papers in her hand, sat on the steps in the entryway of the coffee shop, and sobbed.

After a few minutes, she found her resolve and reread the report. Her shoulders stiffened, and heat rose within her with each word. She would challenge this. *No, challenge isn't strong enough. I'll fight this. I'll fight this, and I'll win!* Sonja tucked the report and check back into the envelope. She needed to think. She wouldn't cash the check until she had looked into the matter. "Cashing it would be an act of acceptance." Sonja put the envelope in a drawer in the nightstand by her bed.

After a restless night of trying to sleep, Sonja finally drifted off for a couple of hours before Damon arrived. He made the coffee and started setting up the counter while Sonja showered. The water cleared her head. She wouldn't say anything to Damon about the insurance check. She had told him she was expecting it, though; so when he asked about it after they closed the shop, her resolve melted.

"They sent a letter. They're not going to pay the full amount. The money I'm supposed to get." Her voice grew louder. "I pay insurance. According to my plan, I've more than met the deductible." Sonja slumped into an empty chair. "I want to fight it, but I don't know what to do."

"I do." Damon's voice was calm. "Get a lawyer. A good lawyer will know exactly what to do. Probably write a strong letter. You have no idea what a strong letter on the letterhead of a big firm can do."

"The only lawyer I know is the guy my realtor recommended to represent me at the closing when I bought this place."

"Call him. If he doesn't handle this kind of stuff, he'll know somebody."

"I'll call him tomorrow and maybe call my dad. He's smart about this kind of stuff."

"I thought he was a gardener or something."

Sonja clenched her fist in her lap, her fingernails digging deep into her palms. "Dad? He owns a landscaping business."

"I didn't mean to insult you. Or your dad. I just mean, I think you should maybe try to call the lawyer first. In the end, it's your shop. Your decision."

Sonja shrugged her shoulders. "I guess you're right." Damon supported her notion of fighting the insurance company. *I am an adult, after all. Time to stop running to Daddy.*

"Hey, cheer up, Sonny Girl. Aren't we supposed to be at someplace called Grady's?

"The fish boil!"

"So, what is this fish boil thing we're going to anyway," Damon asked.

"It's a dining experience," Sonja replied, a twinkle in her eye. "They build a big, wood fire out in back of the restaurant and put a pot over it with red potatoes and chunks of whitefish and cook it until it boils over."

"Great." Damon rolled his eyes.

"No, really. It's fun! Everyone cheers at the boil-over, and the food is great. You'll love it. It's a true Door County experience."

Damon reluctantly pulled his windbreaker over his head. "Wanna take the Harley?"

"No need. We can walk." Sonja was anxious to show Damon around Fish Creek.

"Oh, this keeps getting better and better."

Damon's monotone response didn't dampen Sonja's newfound peace. *A plan. We have a plan. I don't need to call my dad. I have Damon. And a fish boil. And tomorrow, I'll have a lawyer.*

The restaurant was less than a mile away, so they walked down Main Street acting like tourists, stopping only to take in the colorful displays of local vendors. The two arrived about a half hour early at the log building that housed Grady's Bar and Grill. Patrons of the restaurant were already standing out in the backyard of the structure, drinks in hand.

"Okay. You were right," Damon conceded. "The food is delicious, and it is quite an experience."

"All of Door County is an experience," Sonja teased.

"The Chamber of Commerce should hire you."

Arm-in-arm, the couple strolled back to Libby's. Damon stopped at a corner vendor and purchased two ice cream cones.

"A perfect date night." Sonja licked to catch a dribble of chocolate as it made its way down the cone.

A small, blue Honda was parked on the street in front of Libby's.

"Rose!" It was only on seeing the young librarian's car that she remembered the plans she and her friend had made for the evening. She raced ahead to find Rose sitting on the porch.

"What happened?" Rose asked. "I was getting worried. Your car was here; the front door was open; but you were nowhere to be found."

"The front door was open? I thought we locked it." Sonja looked past Rose to the front door. "I'm so sorry. I forgot we made plans. A friend came into town, and I . . . "

By this time, Damon was walking up the sidewalk.

"Hello there," he called out. "Everything okay?"

"Rose, I want you to meet my friend, Damon Evans. Damon, this is my friend, Rose."

"Not Damon Evans, the writer I've heard so much about?" Rose inquired as she extended her hand to the smiling man.

"That would be me," he answered, feigning a bit of modesty Sonja knew didn't exist. He was going to be famous. He had every right to be proud.

"Rose is our librarian," Sonja informed him.

He accepted Rose's extended hand. "You certainly don't look like a librarian. I take it my showing up interrupted plans the two of you had made."

"Oh, it's not a big deal, right, Rose?" Sonja raised her eyebrows and forced a smile. "We were going to a wine and cheese party one of the vineyards is hosting for the locals."

"Is it too late?" Damon asked.

"We could all go," Rose said.

Sonja wasn't sure she wanted to go as a threesome to the party but could hardly say no. She had promised to go with Rose long before Damon had arrived. The evening had been beautiful. Sonja didn't relish spoiling the mood. Still, it was only one night, and Damon seemed interested in going. This was another chance to show him what an interesting place Door County could be.

The three packed into Rose's car. It was a small Honda with limited leg room in the back seat, so Sonja volunteered to sit in the back and let Damon sit in the passenger seat by Rose. The winery was located just off the highway toward Sturgeon Bay.

The backseat left Sonja awkward and uncomfortable. She had to lean forward to hear the conversation. Rose asked about the book Damon was writing. He was sharing the storyline and talking about what his publisher wanted or what his agent said about it. Sonja had heard it before. She relaxed.

"It was Sonja's idea," Damon said, reaching back to touch her hand.

Sonja leaned forward in her seat. "What? What was my idea?"

"I was telling Rose about your idea to move the terrorist strike to Chicago. My publisher thinks it has all sorts of possibilities. Everyone writes about New York City. This could be new. Fresh."

"But I don't like the idea of having the bad guys hide out in Door County," Rose complained. "People might get the wrong idea about us."

"Don't worry. I never have to mention the name of this beautiful place. I can make it someplace just as remote," Damon offered.

Though Rose seemed pleased with the idea, it disturbed Sonja. Damon thought of Door County as remote? After they married, would he want to live someplace else? Wouldn't they live in Fish Creek and have a life like Libby and Joe? Live at the shop? Meet new people? Listen in on the lives of locals as they stopped by for breakfast or lunch? Joan and Craig Linder had carved out a nice life for their family in Fish Creek. Others did it. *Why not us?*

It was Sonja's dream. But was it Damon's?

CHAPTER 18

"SONJA? IT'S CASSIE. GUESS WHAT? I got accepted into the summer study program at the University of Wisconsin in Madison!"

"That's great, Cass!"

"Yeah, but, it means I'll be spending six weeks this summer on campus. I'll earn six college credits, though, so that's cool."

Six weeks in Madison? Sonja glanced at Damon as he washed the dishes. By the end of May, customers coming through Libby's would be steady, and traffic would increase even more after school was out for the summer.

"I think that's wonderful, Cass. Very cool."

"I'll be around to help after school for a while and the first two weeks in the summer, if you still want me."

"That would be perfect. It will at least give me time to find a replacement." Damon was now at the counter, smiling and laughing with one of the locals. "I mean, if it's necessary."

"I can stay as long as you like," Damon told her when she explained the situation. The second week he was there, he single-handedly washed every window in the building inside and out. He fixed the hinge on the screen door and measured the pass-through for a new countertop, even though Sonja said she couldn't afford one.

Two days later, a gruff-looking, heavyset man arrived with a granite countertop. He and Damon muscled it in after deconstructing the old counter, moving the cabinet in the kitchen, and then adding some new wood framing to the area. Damon told her he had done a bit of horse-trading to get it. Sonja wondered what he had to trade, but all he told her was that it's all in making the right connections. Although she would have done the installation after hours or in the off-season and although she would have preferred a more earthy color, Sonja had to agree the counter looked beautiful once it was in place.

"Damon shows so much interest in the shop," she told Fran when she called the next day.

"He sounds too good to be true," Fran said. "Ask him if he has a brother."

Sonja laughed. "The granite countertop he installed looks beautiful, but I lost a lot of kitchen cabinet space. He had to take out the end cabinet."

"Is that all that bad?"

"Kind of. Maybe not. Damon put the old cabinet on the service porch for now, and he's designed an island on locking wheels that'll give me even more room and flexibility. He's going to build it himself as soon as he finds the right wood. He said the wood they sell here isn't high enough quality."

"You are so lucky," Fran said.

"I know." *I'm the luckiest woman in the world. Damon has so many talents. He could do anything and be anywhere, but he chooses to be here with me.* Sonja's heart raced.

Each evening, Sonja made dinner for the two of them.

"It's the least I can do," she told him. "I guess I could pay you what I paid Cassie."

"I'd feel funny taking pay from you. Dinner's good. I've been getting by. Look, we do need to talk about something, though." Damon stirred his meatloaf in the mashed potatoes. "I know you can't pay me. I don't want you to. But soon, I'm going to run out of money. I can't keep living at the B&B. We need to talk about our future."

What he was implying? Was he going to propose? He's never told me he loved me. Well, he had never said the words. But he had come to my rescue. He'd sacrificed everything for me, right? Isn't that love?

"So, I was thinking I could stay here. I help you out, and you give me a room. I'll have more time to work on my book that way; and as soon as my book is done, I'll have more time for the things I really want in life." Damon put his hand over hers. "Sonja, I want what's best for you. I want what's best for *us*."

"I need to think about it, I guess. I mean, I know you're right, but . . . " Sonja hesitated. What was the problem? Damon had been a perfect gentleman. They were both adults. It wasn't like they would be living together. It was more like having a roommate. A very hard-working, good-looking roommate. Why was she hesitant?

Damon moved across the kitchen and leaned against the counter, his arms crossed in front of him. "I guess I could get a job somewhere and come help you when I can. Of course, I don't know how that might affect my writing."

Sonja fidgeted. "How is your book coming?"

"Not so great, I'm afraid. I want to be here with you. I need to be here. I get here in the morning and usually don't leave until after dark." Damon stood and began pacing. He stopped and looked somberly at Sonja, studying her face.

"I hadn't really thought about it like that," Sonja confessed. "I'm terrible!"

"You know how I feel about you," Damon said softly, drawing her up into his arms.

"I know, but . . ." *But do I know?*

He kissed her gently, and the thoughts slipped from her mind.

* * *

The second week of June was the busiest yet. Although Sonja had her misgivings about Damon moving in, he had already set up his room, and she had to admit it was much easier having him in the loft.

Sonja was disappointed when Cassie called to say she wouldn't be able to work at the coffee shop after all. Now was when Sonja needed her most. She and Damon could keep everything running. The hours would be intense. Having Cassie in the afternoons would have given them a much-needed break.

"Not even for an hour a day? I could really use you," Sonja nearly begged.

Cassie seemed vague when she told Sonja she couldn't come at all. Sonja began to suspect it was more than a need to get ready for her excursion to the university. She decided to talk to Joan about it the next chance she had. The opportunity came sooner than expected.

At least once a week, Sonja took a plate of fresh-baked cookies or muffins to Mrs. Atchinson. A ritual between the two women had developed. Sonja would knock on the door, call out in a loud voice to announce what she had baked, set the plate down on the bistro table, and turn to leave. When she neared the gate, the door would open, and Mrs. Atchinson would appear, offer a word of wisdom, then snatch up the baked goods and go back inside. This day was no different.

"Mrs. Atchinson," Sonja called out loudly as she knocked. "It's Sonja. I brought you some cherry chip muffins."

She waited a moment before placing the muffins on the table and turning to leave. Sonja hoped one day she would meet Mrs. Atchinson face-to-face. Obviously, it wasn't going to be today. She had taken a few steps down the walkway when Mrs. Atchinson opened the door and called out.

"That one on the motorbike. That one's not a good man," she called out.

Sonja just waved. *Humph! Mrs. Atchinson hasn't even met Damon. How could she say that?* Sonja walked on. She was about to cross the street when she looked up and saw Joan Linder standing at the corner talking with Patty Elston. Patty, nearing delivery of her first child, looked much like one of the bulbous glass vases her husband created. Sonja stifled a giggle and approached the pair.

"Hi there, girls," she called out. "How are you feeling, Patty?"

After a few minutes of superficial conversation, Patty excused herself to go inside.

"I best be getting back myself," Joan said.

"Okay, but first I need to ask you something. Is Cassie alright? I mean, she planned to work for me some; but when I talked to her the other day, she was . . . I don't know . . . she sounded funny."

Joan looked down and kicked a twig from the sidewalk as Sonja spoke, then drew herself up and looked her squarely in the eye. "What you do is your choice, but I'm Cassie's mother. I'm responsible for her."

"I don't understand," Sonja answered honestly.

"Word has it that man is living with you."

"Damon? Oh, Joan, it's not what you think. He's the one I met in Colorado. Remember? I told you about him that day we went to Green Bay."

"I know who he is."

"He's helping me out. Anyway, we're getting married as soon as he finishes his book."

"But you're not married yet. Try to see it from my point of view. If I just wave this off, my daughter will get the idea I think it's okay for people who aren't married to live together."

"I would never do anything . . . " Sonja's cheeks grew hot. "I'm sorry if you think I would in some way . . . " She didn't know how to finish the sentence. If she didn't leave now, she would cry.

Sonja turned on her heel and headed toward the shop. She heard Joan say something about still being friends but chose not to respond. Tears were burning her eyes by the time she got to Libby's. Instead of running the risk of meeting any customers who may have wandered in during her absence, she slipped around to the rear of the building and entered her apartment door.

Who does she think she is? Judgmental. That's it. One of those judgmental Christians who claim to love everyone but who, without even meeting Damon, had passed judgment on him. Mrs. Atchinson, too. What did that old woman know? Maybe Damon and I won't live here after all. Not with all these hateful people.

Sonja's thoughts flew back to her senior year in high school. A turning point. She had befriended a girl at school, even brought her to church. Ann lived in a trailer park with her mom. Kids from church weren't allowed to go to her house. Even Sonja's parents were hesitant.

They insisted on meeting Ann's mother first. Judgmental. Deciding what a person is by where they live.

The problem was, Sonja knew her own parents wouldn't understand why Damon was living at Libby's Cuppa Joe either. They weren't like the others. Still, she hadn't told them much. Only that Damon had come to help. When she told them he was staying in Sister Creek, she could almost hear her mother's sigh of relief over the phone. When he moved to the apartment, she didn't offer the update.

After washing her face, Sonja returned to the coffee shop to find Damon serving warm muffins to three women who had come in for tea. He finished and rushed to the kitchen, where Sonja stood at the counter mixing a bowl of pimento salad.

"What's wrong? You look like you've been crying."

"Nothing. Everything. Joan Linder won't let Cassie work here because you've moved in."

"Did you tell her we're not exactly living together?"

"They're all a bunch of judgmental, mean people here! She's poisoned everybody against us. I bet she told Mrs. Atchinson, and that's probably what she and Patty Elston were talking about." Sonja bit her lip. *It's probably why Rose hasn't been around either.*

Damon put his arms around her. "Those people don't matter. We matter. All I ever want is for you to be happy."

The next week went by quickly as summer vacationers came in droves to the beckoning shores of Lake Michigan. Sonja was happy. She had, with Damon's help, managed to put aside Joan's comments. "Why should I care what anyone thinks?" she told Damon one afternoon.

"Exactly. We're the only ones that matter. You and me." Damon drew her close. "You're the most important thing in my life."

After closing, Sonja looked around the quiet coffee shop. *Damon is a good man.* She silently acknowledged her success this season was due in large part to Damon. Sonja turned off the lights to the coffee shop and headed downstairs. Damon had showered and now stood in the kitchen making grilled cheese sandwiches.

"Thought I'd treat my girl to my specialty," he announced. Sonja moved closer, and Damon put his arms around her. He smelled good. Fresh and clean. Damon drew her close. As the cheese sandwich toasted, Damon kissed her. Gently. Sonja felt her resolve ebbing away.

* * *

Thursday's crowd was so busy, Sonja had to wait until the evening to finish her baking. Damon left as soon as the doors were officially closed. He often did that when he needed to get away to refresh his creative juices. He told her he found some of his best writing was done sitting by the water.

Sonja fell asleep on the couch waiting for Damon to return. He didn't. In the morning, Sonja opened the coffee shop alone. She was worried. She tried his cell phone but got only his voicemail. She considered calling the sheriff's department. She made the coffee and completed the counter setup. *Surely, he'll be walking through the doors soon.* A week earlier, he had stayed out until two in the morning. He said he was on such a roll, he couldn't stop writing.

"So, where's Damon?" one of the locals asked.

"Writing." Sonja was excited to think his book was nearly finished. Then their life together could really begin. Sonja dropped the man's coffee money in the cash box. She put a fresh batch of blueberry muffins in the oven and set the cookies out under the domed cake plate.

The bell rang above the door. Sonja looked up expectantly. Three young adults—two women and a man—appeared at the counter. Sonja poured their coffee and promised them fresh-baked muffins in three minutes. The man handed her a twenty-dollar bill. Sonja pulled the cash box from under the counter to give him his change. He waited as Sonja stared at the cash box. She counted and recounted the money. Forty-three dollars. Sixty-three with the twenty she held in her hand.

"Ma'am?" the man asked. "Uh, I gave you a twenty."

Sonja was shaking. She gave the young man his change. The timer for the oven sounded. Sonja plated the muffins and delivered them to the three early morning customers now sitting at a table near the bookshelves. She ran hastily back into the kitchen. She had not made it to the bank yesterday. There should have been over three hundred dollars in the box. Her mind was racing.

Maybe Damon put it somewhere safe. He often commented on how anyone could just walk in and take a cash box while they were busy. Sonja searched the kitchen. The money was nowhere to be found. Another couple came into the store. Sonja served them quickly, then stole away to her apartment. She looked in the drawer in Damon's bedside table. Nothing. Perhaps he put the money in one of the drawers where he kept his clothes. Nothing.

Nothing. Not even his clothes. Sonja's stomach began to churn. Sonja squeezed her eyes shut. She felt her self shaking. *What have I done?*

CHAPTER 19

BUSINESS WAS BOOMING. SONJA NEEDED to stay focused on her customers. She tried calling Damon's cell throughout the day but to no avail. He either had it turned off or was ignoring her calls. Sonja's disappointment grew into anger. *I wish I could cry or scream. Or both.* But she didn't have time. During the season, she often stayed open later on Friday evenings; this was one Friday Libby's Cuppa Joe would be closing early.

She hung the "Closed" sign on the door, grabbed the mail from her mailbox on the porch, and locked up. Bills, a letter from the lawyer she had sent her insurance information to, and a plain envelope with just her name scrawled across the front. She recognized the handwriting.

Hey, got a gig in California. Thanks for the hospitality. Took a little "back pay." Catch you next time I'm in Wisconsin. Love, Damon.

Libby's Cuppa Joe was closed on Saturday. Several customers at Dewey's Bait and Tackle made note of it, complaining they hadn't had their morning cup of coffee. Joan tried to call Sonja but got no answer. Joan armed herself with a pot of soup and headed to the coffee shop.

Sonja heard the knocking on the back door, the entrance to her apartment. She wanted to ignore it; but when she heard Joan's voice, she looked out the window.

"Sonja, I know you're in there. I brought you some chicken soup."

Wearily, Sonja opened the door a bit. "I don't feel much like company."

"I knew you must be sick if you didn't open this morning." Joan pushed past the startled young woman.

Sonja knew she looked sick. Her hair was a mess. Her eyes were puffy. She was tired.

"Look at you. You look awful."

Sonja glanced at her reflection in the microwave door. Her terry robe was hanging loosely around her, its long belt trailing after her like the tail of a cat. She tied the belt.

"Sit down and let me get you some soup," Joan ordered.

Sonja plopped down in one of the kitchen chairs, while Joan retrieved a bowl and spoon from Sonja's kitchen. She ladled the soup into the bowl, placed it in front of Sonja, and sat down next to her.

"What's wrong? Is it the flu?" Joan asked as she put her hand to Sonja's forehead just as Annette had done dozens of times when Sonja was a child. "You don't feel hot."

"I . . . I . . . I'm not sick."

"Then, honey, what's wrong?"

Sonja pulled the crumpled note from the pocket of her robe and handed it to Joan. She watched as Joan read the words. Words Sonja had read so many times, she had committed them to memory. Words she read each time, hoping they would somehow change.

"He left?"

Sonja nodded. How could she explain? She didn't want to tell anyone. She didn't want to cry. But there it was. He left her. Damon was gone. The tears and words came gushing out like the water from her broken pipes. Her painful story flooded the room.

"And the funny thing is, I was always so careful to not push him. My friend in Colorado warned me to not tell him I loved him. But I did. Wednesday night, I told him I loved him. I practically proposed to him!" She stopped the story there. She didn't want to tell Joan what happened next.

"When did he leave?" Joan asked.

"Thursday after we closed."

"What's this in the note about 'back pay'?"

"Three hundred dollars. He took it from the cash box." Sonja put her hand over her mouth.

"He stole your money? Did you call the sheriff?"

"No! I'm not telling anyone. Only you. Please don't tell. I feel so stupid."

"You're not stupid. Foolish? Yes. Stupid? No."

Sonja looked at her friend. Joan smiled. "Okay. I'm foolish."

"It happens. Some men have a way of getting what they want without giving us what we want or need. It's been going on for centuries. You're not the first girl to trust your heart to an untrustworthy man."

"You knew, didn't you? You knew that day out on the street."

"I didn't know Damon. I met him only once or twice. I just knew you were in a bad situation, that's all." Joan pushed the bowl closer to Sonja. "Here, eat some soup. It really will make you feel better."

Joan did more than bring soup. She brought care and love. Sonja appreciated having Joan Linder as a friend. *Maybe I was the one being a bit judgmental.*

Joan stood to leave. "Get dressed. You'll feel better. We're driving Cassie to Madison tomorrow; but we'll be back tomorrow night, and I'll come help you Monday morning."

"You are such a good friend, Joan. And actually, the following week, my mom might come. I told her I didn't know if I would need her. She was taking some workshop for teaching math. I think it's over soon. Maybe she'll come."

Maybe she would come. Maybe Sonja would ask. Sonja wasn't sure what she would tell her mother. She wasn't sure she would call. She knew she wouldn't call until she was in a better frame of mind, anyway.

* * *

Annette Parker cleared the table and stuffed the dollar bill she found on it in the tip jar on the counter. "This is fun! Most of my friends in high school had jobs at restaurants or fast food places. I never got to do that. I always worked for my dad on our farm in the summer."

"I'm glad you could come. The Fourth of July is always busy."

"I'm glad I can help. I know Cassie's doing that college class, but what happened to that friend of yours from Colorado?"

"Damon? Oh, he left. He was only in Door County for a few weeks. It was good to have him help out a bit, though, since Cassie couldn't."

"You've carved out such a good life here. Your dad and I are so proud of you."

If you only knew, Mom.

The lawyer she consulted said she didn't have a case. The man she thought she would spend the rest of her life with had stolen much-needed money from her and left town. And now, she was getting sick.

She was edgy and uncomfortable. For the past two days, she had not eaten much; and when she did, she couldn't keep her food down. So far, she'd been able to hide her illness from her mother. The last thing she wanted right now was her mother smothering her with well-intended care. Sonja actually felt best when she was working and interacting with the customers. She let her mother virtually take over the kitchen. She didn't think it wise to handle the food, even if she did use gloves. No need for anyone else to catch what she had.

By the week's end, Sonja had come to the realization no one was likely to catch what she had. She would wait until her parents left, then get one of those tests she could perform on her own at home. She couldn't sleep. She tossed and turned all night. If this "illness" turned out to be what she thought it might be, how could she ever face her parents again? What would she tell Joan or Rose?

How can I tell Damon? Will I tell him? Damon had ended the relationship. *Thanks for the hospitality.* She hadn't called him then, and she wouldn't call him now. *Hospitality. Humph! If only I had listened to Mrs. Atchinson. No, I can't blame it all on Damon. I'm the one who wanted love. Wanted a relationship. I'm the one who should have said no.*

CHAPTER 20

AN OBSTETRICIAN IN STURGEON BAY confirmed what she already knew. He told her she could expect to deliver on or about March twelfth. Sonja wanted to be happy, but she wasn't. She couldn't come to terms with the fact she had gone about things backwards.

"Oh, Joan, how can I face my parents? What if they can't—or won't—forgive me? I can't even forgive myself."

"Don't sell your parents short. You need to tell them—and soon. This isn't something you can exactly hide."

Sonja squirmed. "I hate the idea of disappointing them."

Joan patted Sonja's hand. "I can imagine. But Sonja, there are worse things. You told me. That's a start."

"Like practice." Sonja sighed. "I guess I better practice with Rose, too. We haven't talked in weeks."

It was the first week of August before Sonja finally found the courage to approach Rose. The library was open all day during the season, but Sonja couldn't imagine it to be such consuming work Rose hadn't stopped by at all. She chose a slow Wednesday afternoon to close for an hour and venture down the street to the library.

Rose jerked her head up when Sonja walked through the door. She turned to her computer and began typing the number of the book she had just added to the stacks. There was no one in the library at the time. It would be hard to avoid a conversation.

"Hi there, Rose."

"Hey." Rose didn't look up.

"Busy?"

"Got a bunch of books donated. I have to get them in the system." Rose continued to type.

"Any way you could take a break? I really need to talk to you."

Rose's lip quivered. She turned to Sonja, clearly shaken. She had tears in her eyes.

"Honest, Sonja, I had no idea. I told him no. I told him you and I are friends. Nothing happened," Rose cried.

Sonja stood silently next to the counter Rose used to check books in and out of the library. "Damon." It was not a question.

"He sometimes came by. He said he could write better here where it was quiet. But honest, Sonja, I did not in any way encourage him. And he hasn't been by for a long time now."

Sonja sat down on a stool near the counter. A picture of Damon flirting with Rose in the car on the night they all went to the wine and cheese party filled her mind. "He's gone."

"I'm so sorry, Sonja. I never . . . "

"It wasn't you," Sonja assured Rose. "And it wasn't me, either, I guess. It was him."

Rose came around from behind the counter and hugged Sonja. "I'm so sorry."

Sonja offered a weak smile. "I still need to talk to you."

The two women sat down in the quiet of the library. Sonja rubbed her hands together. Her story came out in spurts.

"What about adoption?" Rose asked when Sonja told her the news.

Sonja shook her head. "Give the child away and go on with my life as if he or she never existed? I just don't see how I could do that. Maybe if I was some young teenager. This baby is my responsibility."

"I should have told you about him coming on to me sooner. Maybe then you would have broken it off."

"Hah! I probably would have accused you of making it up or something. I couldn't see Damon for who he was."

"Or wasn't. I don't think he was a writer, either. Did you ever look in that notebook he carried?" Sonja shook her head, so Rose continued, "I peeked once when he left it on the table and went to the bathroom."

"And?"

"And it had a bunch of different stuff in it. Lists of things, addresses, a lot of doodling, and a letter started to someone named Lynn."

"He was a fraud in every way," Sonja admitted reluctantly.

"Have you talked with your folks about this?"

"No. What do I tell them?"

"The truth."

What was the truth? She was twenty-nine years old. She wavered between "I am an adult," and "I made a mistake." *I am an adult who made a mistake. A big mistake.*

She would never tell this child that he or she was a mistake. The list of errors in her life was long. Her mind tumbled them over in a fit of painful guilt.

I selfishly sought a relationship that turned out to be one-sided, even though I had been warned and the signs were there. I let down my guard and ignored the teaching of my childhood.

"What truth, Rose? That I yielded to my emotions of the present without any thought to what it might mean for the future or, now, the future of a child? This is going to hurt them."

"It could be worse," Rose said.

"That's what Joan told me. I'll tell them, but the big question now is when?"

"Not over the phone."

"I know. I guess it'll have to be after the pumpkin festival. They're expecting me then. I just don't know if it's fair to wait that long."

"My sister-in-law didn't tell us about Lucas until after the first trimester. She said most miscarriages occur in that timeframe, and she wanted to be sure."

Sonja did the math. *I'll be in my twelfth week in mid-September. The pumpkin festival is the first week in October.* "I guess that settles it."

* * *

Everyone in the county had a theory as to why the attendance at the annual pumpkin festival held in Egg Harbor was down.

"It's an election year," some offered over their breakfast coffee. "Always down in an election year."

"It's the economy," others suggested. "The economy is taking a dip, and people don't want to spend money on a weekend vacation."

The reason for lower attendance didn't matter. In truth, the summer season had been very strong, so most businesses looked at the revenue from the festival as icing on the cake. Libby's didn't show a dip at all. Sonja's pumpkin spice muffins with streusel topping were so popular, she had to bake multiple batches every day.

This year, however, once the festival was over, Sonja took an extra week to close Libby's Cuppa Joe. She was in no hurry.

She scrubbed everything, cleaned out the refrigerators in both kitchens. Though she now knew how to appropriately close everything down for the winter, she wouldn't need to this year. She would go to Kenosha but return shortly thereafter.

"Everything is going to be okay," Joan Linder told her as Sonja handed her a key to the shop. "We'll keep an eye on things."

"And I'm praying for you, too," Cassie said. She offered Sonja a side hug.

It was sweet. Maybe it would help if someone like Cassie prayed. *I'm certainly doubtful, God, that You want to hear any prayers from me right now.*

Sonja called her parents to let them know she was not going back to Colorado this year during the winter season, but she didn't offer a reason for the choice to stay in Wisconsin. "I was hoping I could maybe stay with you through Thanksgiving."

"Afraid to leave the shop over the winter again?" Daniel asked.

"You can stay with us as long as you like," Annette said.

How would they feel when she finally gathered up the courage to tell them everything?

Stopping in Green Bay for a few hours was an easy decision. Sonja did not look forward to this trip to Kenosha, so a visit with Joe was a welcome distraction.

Joe held the picture in his hand. A tear came to his eyes. Sonja began to wonder if she was right in bringing the photo to the old man.

"I found it in a cookbook," she shared.

"Judy and Joey," the old man managed to say, his finger gently touching the faces on the picture. "He was only sixteen, you know. Judy never forgave herself."

Sonja put her hand on his trembling shoulder. She looked at his frail hand holding tightly to a memory. A memory that caused him pain. A memory about which she knew nothing.

Joe's eyes filled with tears. "Judy? Is that you?"

"It's Sonja, Joe. Remember? From the coffee shop."

Joe turned his head away, lost in the past. *Now what? Slip out quietly? Maybe I should get somebody. A nurse.* Sonja reached to pat his hand and tell him she needed to leave. Joe took her hand in his and held tightly.

"Judy, I want to go home. I just want to go home. I want things to be right again."

Sonja swallowed hard and managed to gently pull from his grasp. She tiptoed out of the room and found a nurse's aide.

"Hi. I was just in to see Joe Davis. I'm afraid he is very upset. Do you think you could call his daughter? Maybe she could come by or something," Sonja asked the aide.

"Mr. Joe? I'll check on him." The aide was wearing scrubs with little clowns on them. Sonja thought she belonged in a children's ward instead of working with older people like Joe.

But wasn't that what she had thought before? That the people here tended to talk down to the residents as if they were children instead of men and women who had led interesting lives and deserved some respect. Sonja went back to Joe.

"Hi, Joe. It's me, Sonja, the woman who bought your coffee shop," she said brightly as she entered his room.

"Oh, yes," Joe smiled. "Where did you take off to?"

Sonja smiled and asked if he would like another sugar-free cookie.

The picture rested on his lap. Someone had mentioned before that Joe had a daughter, but no one spoke of Joey. A son? Sonja could see the resemblance. Joey was a young version of the man sitting before her today. The square jaw. The wide smile. Whatever happened to Joey, it was not good. Mrs. Atchinson probably could tell her—if she could ever sit down and have a real conversation with the woman. Maybe Joan or Craig Linder knew.

"I have a long drive to Kenosha, so I probably should head out."

Joe nodded. "Everything is going to work out just fine for you, Sonja. Trust God, and He will see you through all of this."

Did he know? How? Flustered, Sonja left the room and flew down the hall to the elevator. She hadn't told Joe about the baby or Damon. She hadn't told him about the flooding of Libby's or anything. Yet somehow, he knew. Or at least he knew something was troubling her. That was it. Joe knew something was troubling her. And what was it he said? "Everything is going to work out just fine for you, Sonja."

Would her father be as gentle? Would everything really work out? Did God care?

CHAPTER 21

DANIEL PARKER STACKED THE FIREWOOD up beside the garage. Sonja wanted to help, but he waved her off. Instead, she found herself watching him from the kitchen window, while her mother busied herself with cutting vegetables for the stew she was preparing that night.

"Daddy's disappointed in me."

"We suspected, but we were both shocked at the same time," Annette told her daughter. "Your dad just needs time to digest this. You know him. He does his best thinking and praying when he's outside working."

The three had been up into the wee hours of the morning. Daniel wanted to know who the father was and why he wasn't around now. Annette was more interested in how Sonja was faring physically. It was a hard conversation to have.

Sonja turned from the window. "You suspected?"

"Yes. And no. You were sick every morning when I was up there, just like I was with you. I knew that boy had been there. The one you met in Colorado. I just prayed I was wrong."

Sonja folded her arms tight around her body, chilled with the pain she saw in her mother's eyes. That boy, as her mother called Damon, was a thirty-two-year-old adolescent pretending to be a man. Her father called him a jerk. Sonja understood. She had often thought of him as a jerk herself. But then she thought of the child growing inside her.

No matter what else Damon Evans was or was not, he was the father of this baby. It would be hard to keep that perspective.

If it weren't for the few extra pounds, she wouldn't feel pregnant at all. But she was. Sonja wandered around the house trying to sort through her life. Other women managed to raise a child and work at the same time. Her own mother had been a teacher for as long as Sonja remembered. *Of course, she had a husband to help.*

She retrieved the photo album her mother had used to chronicle Sonja's childhood and sank into the big, soft, green leather chair in the den, the book in hand.

The album started with what Sonja had always called the "chair pictures." A series of six pictures stared up at her. Six of her closest relatives, each taking their turn holding baby Sonja, while sitting in a plaid wing-backed chair. Sonja touched each face with love. There was her father, holding her stiffly with a huge grin on his face. Her Grandma Bess was next. Sonja smiled at the hat her paternal grandmother donned for the occasion. Then there was the picture of her Grandpa Ray, her paternal grandfather sitting in the chair, holding his first grandchild even more stiffly than his son. On the opposite page, a young Annette sat in the designated chair looking lovingly at the newborn baby in her arms. Beneath her photo were her parents, Sonja's maternal grandparents. Grandpa Jim sat tall and straight, not really holding baby Sonja. He sort of let her balance on his lap, one strong hand cradling her head. And then there was Grandma Grace.

Sonja was always closest to Grandma Grace. In part, because like Annette, Grandma Grace had been a teacher. She loved to get down on the floor and play with her granddaughter. She took time to teach Sonja how to do things. Things like drawing or crocheting. She taught Sonja how to play the piano. Every summer, Grandma Grace and Grandpa Jim took Sonja with them for a week or two to stay with them on the farm. She would help them in the garden and swing on the plank board swing Grandpa Jim put up in the big oak tree in the front yard. After Grandpa Jim died, Grandma Grace came to live with the Parker family.

Tears were stinging Sonja's eyes as she gently touched the picture of Grandma Grace sitting in that awful plaid chair, holding Sonja close. *I have so let you down, Grandma Grace.*

Sonja thought she would one day have a loving husband like Grandpa Jim or like her own dad. *Isn't that what I thought? That Damon cared for me and respected me the way Dad cared for and respected Mom?* But unlike her father, Damon was a liar. He had played on her emotions. He had toyed with her heart. Her eyes burned. Sonja rested her head against the back of the chair and closed her eyes.

Sonja didn't realize she had fallen asleep, the album on her lap, until she heard her father's voice. He leaned over and kissed her forehead.

"Sonja?" Daniel whispered. "Are you okay, honey?"

Sonja sat up and rubbed her puffy eyes. "I must have dozed off."

"Sweetheart, can we talk?"

"Of course, Daddy." Fully awake now, she was keenly aware of the subject at hand. "Oh, Dad, I'm so sorry I've disappointed you."

"Shhh," Daniel said quietly. He held her hand in his and patted it. "I've been thinking. You know the Bible says we should praise God in all things. Not *for* all things, mind you, but in them and through them."

Sonja could see the struggle in her father's face. She could also see he had reached a decision. There was a tenderness to his voice she did not expect and was certain she did not deserve.

"I've been thinking a lot about that verse," Daniel said. "I've been thinking a lot about you, too. I want to tell you how proud I am of you."

What?

"I'm proud of you for not making this all worse by having an abortion. You are certainly an adult and could have made that decision, and we would have never known. And after last night, after you expressed your conviction to keep and raise this child . . . well, I don't know, I just wanted you to know that I am proud of you for acting selflessly.

"Sometimes I think young girls keep their babies for selfish reasons. They keep them because they want someone to love them. And sometimes they give them up for adoption for selfish reasons, too—so, they can go on with what they want in life without the burden of raising a child. You want to take responsibility. You want to assure the best for your child. I'm praising God for that." Daniel had tears in his eyes.

"Oh, Daddy." Sonja threw her arms around Daniel's neck. "This time I don't want to just *know* what is right; I want to *pursue* what is right. I can't do that without you and Mom."

"Well, don't go thinking I'm all that great," Daniel warned. "I have a long way to go before I can truly forgive this Damon fellow. I know I have to do that, but it's going to be a process. And there's something else. Your mother and I think you should stay here to see this pregnancy through. I'll go with you to close up Libby's."

* * *

Two days later, once they had passed through the Milwaukee metropolitan area, Sonja asked if they might stop to see Joe Davis in Green Bay. "I want you to meet him."

Joe was in the common room when they arrived. He had just finished his lunch and was talking with another man. Sonja hesitated.

She hated to interrupt, but she and her father had driven several miles out of their way to see him.

Joe made her decision for her when he saw her in the doorway. "There's the gal that's running my business for me!"

For a moment, Sonja considered reminding him that she purchased the store but decided to let the comment pass. Instead, she and her father pulled two chairs over from a nearby table and joined Joe and his friend.

"Joe, this is my father, Daniel Parker." Then turning to Joe's companion, she introduced herself.

"That's a fine girl you raised there, Daniel," Joe said.

"She speaks highly of you as well," Daniel replied.

Joe was in good form. The four talked for a few minutes about the weather and the likelihood of a colder-than-normal winter. Joe's friend, Mr. Withers, claimed he had taken a walk and seen all the signs of a particularly cold winter. His predictions were based on wooly worms and the thickness of the pumpkin shell. When his therapist came for him, he managed slowly to hoist himself up from his dining chair and made his way toward the big double doors with the help of a walker.

"Now there goes a smart man," Joe proclaimed as Mr. Withers walked through the doors.

"So, you think he's right about it being a cold winter?" Sonja asked.

"Much as I can remember, every winter's a cold one." Joe laughed.

Talk turned to Libby's Cuppa Joe. Sonja hadn't told Joe anything about the changes she had made; but when Daniel mentioned the new color on the walls, Joe was interested.

"I remodeled that basement house myself," Joe said. "Used to have three tiny bedrooms. Took me years to talk Libby into it; but once I got it done, she was pretty happy."

"It's a great space," Sonja said. "I like that there is so much light."

"Only way to do up a basement house." Joe was interested in everything they could tell him about the store. He wanted to know what was on the menu and if she ever made kringle. Though Sonja had eaten kringle on many occasions, she had never attempted to make the popular Danish pastry. Daniel told Joe the recipe he had given Sonja for coffee was wonderful.

"The best cup of coffee I've ever had," Daniel said. "I'm not one for all those fancy coffees a lot of places serve now. Just give me a regular cup of joe."

Joe rubbed his chin. "Well, I have to admit, I kinda like some of those fancy coffees. Once, I took Libby to Chicago, and we tried some of those espressos and cappuccinos and such. I tried to get her to add it to the shop, but she wasn't one for change. Maybe you'll get more use outta that machine I bought."

Was Joe suggesting he had purchased an espresso machine? If so, what happened to it? "What machine?" she asked.

"That espresso machine. Top of the line. But she wouldn't have anything to do with it. Just got stored up in the closet."

The storage area under the sloping rooftop was the only one she hadn't fully explored. The couple of boxes near the entrance had Christmas ornaments and personal effects in them. Though she fully intended to clean out the area at some point, she had never been motivated to do so. Now she wondered if, indeed, under everything else, there might be an espresso machine.

"When did you get the espresso machine?" Sonja asked cautiously. She hated to get her hopes up.

"Well, let me see." Joe scratched his head. "Guess we went to Chicago the March before Libby got sick. I ordered it so we could use it that season, but she wasn't inclined to try. Said she would read up on it and practice with it that winter, but then she got sick. Never uncrated the thing; just put it in storage. Thing's brand new, you know."

By the time they left, Sonja had a hard time keeping her excitement in check. She and her dad made a plan to spend their first hours at the shop taking everything out of the storage area. Sonja was glad her father was with her. He would help her with the heavy things. Who knew what else was in the boxes under the roof?

They stopped in Sturgeon Bay for an early dinner, then made their way up the highway to Fish Creek. Dusk was setting in by the time they arrived. Sonja knew the prudent thing to do was to settle in and wait to go through the closet in the morning. Daniel agreed that was the smart thing to do; but seeing the look in his daughter's eyes, he suggested they just pull a few things out into the large open area and at least see if there was an espresso maker in the closet as Joe indicated. Sonja's heart soared.

The first few boxes Daniel carried into the upper room of the coffee shop for Sonja to inspect were exactly what she had expected to find—Christmas decorations, a wooden reindeer for the lawn, and boxes of clothes. The next box was filled with photo albums, newspaper clippings, and an assortment of school pictures and report cards. Sonja wondered if answers to the mystery of Judy and Joey were hidden in the contents of that box. Finally, Daniel let out a loud "yippee" from within the depths of the storage area.

"I found it, Sonja! You are the proud owner of an honest-to-goodness espresso machine," he told his daughter as he emerged triumphantly from the closet, dragging a large crate behind him. "There's a bigger crate and some other boxes from the same company in there. I'll get them. There are more boxes and a few pieces of furniture back in there. Do you want them out, too?"

"Not yet, Dad." Sonja sat on the floor amid the boxes and read the information on the crate in front of her. Joe was right. It was brand new. She took the papers from the plastic bag attached to the outside and began studying the specifics of her trophy. It wasn't the fanciest or biggest or maybe even the best machine by today's standards, but it would be perfect for Libby's. And it was a good brand. A name she trusted. They left the mess they had made on the floor and took the manual and paperwork with them to the living quarters.

Sleep came easier than expected that night. Sonja read the espresso manual from cover to cover before drifting off into a full night of rest. Tomorrow, her dad would set it up for her in the coffee shop kitchen and run the water line to it. Although she was anxious to try it out, just getting it set up at this point was enough. Then they could turn their attention to the job at hand. They had to winterize the building, so it would remain intact through Mr. Wither's predicted harsh weather. This time it would be done right.

Sonja also wanted to clean up the mess they had made in the upper room before returning to Kenosha. She doubted she would feel much like tackling it when she returned. Sonja thought about her return to the shop as she brushed her teeth the next morning. When she returned, she would not be alone. She would have a baby with her. This would be their home. For the first time since realizing she was pregnant, the baby seemed real to her.

CHAPTER 22

DR. LEONARD ASKED IF SHE had felt life yet. "Any movement?" he clarified.

"I'm not sure," Sonja answered honestly. "I felt a few butterflies in my stomach. Maybe."

"Probably the baby. It will often feel like a flutter at first. Let's see if we can hear the heartbeat."

Tears rolled down Sonja's cheeks as the heartbeat, fast and loud, reverberated through the machine. The examination lasted all of ten minutes.

As Sonja made her next appointment at the front desk, the receptionist smiled. "Your first?"

"Yes, and the doctor said he'll do an ultrasound at the next visit."

"Super! You know we used to have to send you to the hospital for that. Now we do them right here in the office. The baby's father can come, too."

Sonja's cheeks warmed as the office aide turned to the file to schedule the appointment. Without missing a beat, she added, "Or whomever you like." Had she read something on the file? Did she see Sonja's embarrassment?

For a long time, Sonja sat in her car. She thought she was ready to be a single mother. But being a single mother meant more than caring for the baby. There was more to it than revealing her pregnancy to her parents and closest friends. For the rest of her life, people would ask about this child's father. Or make assumptions. Or both.

Sonja also realized she had spent the first four months of her pregnancy worrying over how to tell her parents or being angry with Damon. She had spent an inordinate amount of time beating herself up emotionally for what had happened. There was a baby inside her. A living, growing human being. She had been given nine months to prepare for this child and by her own reckoning, she had wasted nearly half of it.

The Kenosha Public library is a fairly large brick building with a decent collection of materials. Sonja walked immediately to one of the computer terminals and located the books she needed. She checked out *What to Expect When You're Expecting,* as well as a book about health and nutrition and one about breastfeeding. Sonja stopped by a department store to check out the baby furniture, clothes, and other necessities.

The baby department was overwhelming. Everything looked cute and interesting; but to purchase everything the store clerk claimed were "must haves," Sonja would need thousands of dollars she didn't have, as well as more room to store everything.

It was time to call her longtime friend, Gina. This would be hard, but Sonja needed someone her age to talk to about baby stuff. Her parents were great, but they didn't have a clue about being pregnant in the twenty-first century.

When Sonja called, Gina invited her over for lunch the next day. Sonja was surprised to learn Gina's two older children were in school.

"Where did that time go? It seems like you and Trevor got married only a couple of years ago."

Gina laughed. "Jason's in third grade, and Gwen's in first. Ellie's my baby, but she'll go to kindergarten next year. Don't know what I'll do then. So how about you? Do you think you'll ever find that special someone, get married, and have a family?"

Sonja squirmed. She clinked the saucer with the side of her fork. "About that."

By the time Sonja finished confiding in her friend, both were in tears.

"What's wrong, Mommy?" Four-year-old Ellie stood at the doorway, her long-sleeved t-shirt covered with colorful stickers.

Gina wiped her eyes and crossed the kitchen to pick up her daughter. "Nothing's wrong, sweetie. I haven't seen my friend in a long time, and we're sort of catching up." She kissed Ellie's cheek and told her to pick up her arts and crafts stuff before her brother and sister got home from school. "We're going to the fall festival at church tonight, so you want to be ready."

Ellie squealed with delight and headed back to her room.

"Sonja, I'm here for you. I just want you to know that. I'll help you, answer questions, whatever you need."

A lump formed in Sonja's throat. "You have no idea what that means to me."

"And I think you should come to church. You'll find a lot of support there, as well."

"I don't know. Maybe. It's hard. I mean some of those people taught me in Sunday school."

"And they'll love you through this. You'll see."

Daniel and Annette did not press Sonja about church, although they did suggest to her it would be harder for her the longer she waited. They strongly suggested she contact Damon, though.

"I don't know, honey," Daniel said. "I just think you should let him know. He is the father, and well, maybe he'll step up and do the right thing."

"I'm not sure he knows what the right thing to do is, Dad. I don't ever want to see him again. Ever."

Annette put her hand over Sonja's. "I understand, sweetheart, but think about the baby. I mean, what if there's a medical need or something? Do you know anything at all about Damon's history?"

Instinctively, Sonja drew her arms around her as if to protect her unborn child. "I never thought about that." Tears spilled down her cheeks. "I'm awful! How will I ever be a good mother?"

Annette put her arms around her daughter and patted her back. "Shhh . . . there, there. You're going to be a wonderful mother. I'm sorry we upset you."

Daniel left the room.

"I've so disappointed you and Daddy. And Mom, honestly, I wouldn't even know how to contact Damon. He never answered his phone after he left. It's as if I never existed to him."

Nothing more was said about Damon Evans. More was said about going to church. Finally, Sonja decided to go with her parents to the Thanksgiving Eve service. This was new. She didn't remember the church offering an evening service on the Wednesday evening before the holiday. *This could be good.*

Unfortunately, the way the program was put together was just like every other gathering the church offered. Sonja thought it was stoic and cold. The music consisted of a series of hymns, one after the other, taken straight from the thick, green hymnals Sonja remembered from her youth. The songs had been placed in the hymnal with the category title "Songs of Thanksgiving" running across the top like the header of a term paper.

"You can't beat some of those old hymns," Annette remarked as they filed out into the vestibule of the church. "I love the words. Some of those I haven't heard in a long time." Sonja fought the urge to roll her eyes and instead looked out to see if there was anyone there she knew. Gratefully, only a few friends of her parents were present. Sonja suspected her mother had shared with them the news of Sonja's pregnancy. Her mother was one to put everything out to a group of women she called her prayer warriors. But if they knew, they didn't say anything. They just greeted Sonja as if she had never left and told her how wonderful it was to see her. One of her mother's closest friends, Diane, asked about the shop and promised she and her husband fully intended to get up to Door County for a vacation next summer.

"Hey there, girl! I hoped I would see you here," came a familiar voice.

Sonja turned. "Hi, Liz. How are you?"

"Great, but I gotta get these munchkins home. I'm in charge of the turkey tomorrow, so I have to get up early."

Sonja looked down at the two children chasing each other, using their mother as a center pole for their antics. "They've really grown."

Liz stooped to put a coat on the youngest, a girl about two years old. Sonja knew Leon was about six. She had been to a shower for Liz when she was expecting him.

Liz stood up. "Hey, listen. I talked to Gina. I want you to know I'm here for you. And I didn't want you guessing who knows and who doesn't. You know what I mean?"

Sonja hadn't sworn Gina to secrecy or anything, and she knew, as Joan had warned, this wasn't something she could keep secret. Liz was being honest with her. She hugged Liz. "Thank you. You don't know what this means to me."

* * *

Because of the holidays, Sonja had to schedule her obstetrician's appointment for the week after Thanksgiving. Hesitantly, she invited both parents to accompany her; but when her father begged off, Sonja was relieved. Annette had to use a half day of personal leave to make the appointment but told Sonja wild horses couldn't keep her away.

"Hi, my name is Patricia. So, I see you're going to have an ultrasound today," the technician said without looking up from Sonja's chart. "If we can see everything, do you want to know what the gender is?"

Sonja looked at her mom. "I think so."

"Well, we'll see what we can do. Of course, the real purpose here is to make sure everything is developing properly for your baby."

Sonja lay down on the examining table. Annette held her hand. Soon, images of the baby were being projected on a large computer screen. Patricia hit the keys on her computer and zoomed in on a particular shot. She explained everything they were seeing.

At first, the images were vague; but once Patricia located the baby's head, both Sonja and Annette let out a little gasp. The outline of a sweet baby was evident. A tiny hand came up by the baby's ear. Tiny fingers opened, then closed again. Neither woman could breathe. A baby. A real baby.

"And there's the heart beating," Patricia said.

"I can't believe we can see the heart!" Annette exclaimed. Sonja could hear the smile in her mother's voice. She would have looked at her directly but couldn't take her eyes off of the child growing inside her.

Patricia looked at the kidneys and other organs. She pointed out the measurements of the appendages that would be of interest to the doctor. She moved the sensor around on Sonja's stomach. The baby was moving, too. "Hmm . . . I don't think we are going to get a good picture here."

"Is something wrong?" Sonja asked.

"No, nothing's wrong. Just can't get the right shot to see if we're looking at a boy or a girl. Wait a minute. Here we go. Do you want to know?"

"Yes. Yes, I want to know."

"Well, I hope you're partial to the color pink."

"A girl!" Annette sighed. "I'm going to have a granddaughter."

A girl. Sonja realized later that was the very moment she stopped thinking about the coffee shop. Libby's Cuppa Joe was nothing. It was a job. A crazy dream. This. This was reality. This was a child. A girl. Her daughter. Her life. Sonja knew fully at that moment, nothing in her life would ever be the same. Nothing.

Christmas came and went with mostly talk about how wonderful next Christmas would be with a little one around. Sonja's arms ached to hold the baby. At an after-Christmas sale, she purchased a needlepoint kit to make the baby a Christmas stocking. She faithfully attended the childbirth classes offered at the hospital. Though it was still awkward, she was surprised to find she wasn't the only single mom there. Annette went with her to the classes.

"I've been thinking about something you and Dad said," Sonja told her mother one evening after class. "Maybe I should tell Damon."

Annette grimaced and shifted her hands on the steering wheel. "I thought that you didn't want anything to do with him."

"I don't want anything to do with him, Mom. It's just that, well, if there was any medical issue, I think I should know about it. And Daddy says he has a right to know."

"I know what your father says. I just hate to think of him coming into your life and hurting you again. I never met the man, and I don't like him! Besides, do you even know how to reach him?"

"I've been thinking about that. He may be back in Steamboat working as a ski instructor."

"You could call your friend. The one we stayed with last Christmas."

Sonja stared through the frosty car window into the dark night. "I've talked to her only a couple of times. Once to tell her I wouldn't be coming this year. I didn't tell her why. And when she called to wish me a Merry Christmas, I froze."

"Just text her."

Texting Cindy proved harder than Sonja imagined. "I can't start with 'Have you seen Damon?'" she told Gina over lunch.

"Start with a sort of 'Hey, how are you?' and chat a bit." Gina took a sip of her water. "In fact, you could just call her."

"I don't want to call. I don't want to be tempted to blurt out, 'By the way, you were right about Damon. Guess what? I'm pregnant!'"

"I can see that."

Sonja pulled out her phone and texted Cindy. "It'll take her a while. She parties late into the night and sleeps late into the day."

"So, what did you settle on?"

Sonja looked at her phone. "I just said, 'If you see Damon, tell him to give me a call.'"

The two friends finished their lunch and headed to a local department store. Gina's insight on what were "must haves" and what you did not need for a baby differed greatly from what store clerks suggested. Sonja was grateful for her advice. Shopping and planning for the baby felt productive—a step in the right direction. Waiting for this little one to hold in her arms was hard. The long winter months passed slowly. Sonja held up a soft baby blanket and realized she was more anxious to hold her baby in her arms than she could have ever imagined.

CHAPTER 23

LATE IN JANUARY, GINA AND Liz, along with a few others from church, threw a baby shower for her. Since she didn't attend church regularly, Sonja didn't expect the party, and the gesture warmed her heart.

Sonja finally reached Cindy at the Rocky Mountain Coffee Bar, and Daniel contacted the ski pro shop. Neither had seen or heard from Damon this season.

"I take it he didn't leave the ski lodge on the best of terms," Daniel told his daughter. "They didn't offer any specifics. They said if we found him to let them know where he is."

Sonja tried to put Damon out of her mind.

The final months of Sonja's pregnancy melted away, even though the winter's snow lingered well into March. The twelfth of March came and went. But her doctor had said "on or about," Sonja reminded herself.

On or about . . .

* * *

"Grace." Annette held out her arms to take the baby the nurse had wrapped in a tiny white blanket. "Hello, little baby Grace."

"Grace Anne after Grandma Grace and you."

Annette's face scrunched—a smile and tears fighting against each other.

Daniel sat down in a chair before allowing Annette to place the bundle of newborn baby in his arms. Sonja had never seen her dad so cautious about anything. He looked into Grace's soft face, then back to his daughter. "She looks just like you when you were born."

Would Grace grow up to look like me or more like Damon? A shiver went down Sonja's spine. *What would happen if Damon came back?* Could she protect her little girl from him? Should she? All she knew for sure at this very moment was that Grace was like a gift. A new beginning to a new life. Sonja watched as her parents held the sleeping child, talking softly in her ear. Whispering words of love and devotion. Words that Sonja knew from experience were trustworthy and would last her a lifetime.

As much as Sonja enjoyed the attention her parents gave both her and the baby, once the infant was a month old, Sonja knew it was time to return to Fish Creek. She would leave immediately after her six-week doctor appointment. Even then, it would be a push to open the store before the end of May. Her resolve to be the responsible adult she knew she should be would diminish if she lingered in Kenosha much longer.

"I understand," Annette said. "I'll come help with the shop as soon as school is out."

Daniel didn't understand. He was reluctant to let his daughter and granddaughter go. "Call it selfish, but I like coming home to you and Grace."

"Well, I have to admit, it's been pretty nice having extra hands to help out, and you turned out to be pretty decent at changing a diaper or two. But I have to go, Dad. Mom said she'll ride up with me and help get us settled, and then you can come for her on Sunday."

"I'll come Saturday night. And I'll be there anytime you need me. I'm a phone call away."

The drive to Door County was made longer due to the need to pull over frequently to feed and change the baby. All the way, Annette recalled trips she and Daniel had made when Sonja was an infant.

"There were no car seat rules then. I can't believe it now, but we thought nothing of me holding you in my arms while your dad drove. Of course, cars were like heavy armored tanks back in those days."

Sonja would like to have stopped to see Joe, but didn't want to take her tiny child into the ward of old, sick people. Maybe later. She told her mother about the old man. "I know he has a daughter, and I think something must have happened to his son. I don't know if he has any grandchildren or not." *But there is that box of stuff in the storage closet.*

Annette interrupted her thoughts. "What do you say we stop for a bite to eat in Sturgeon Bay?"

"Good idea." Sonja took her to a small café on Third Avenue in the historic section of town. Baby Grace was asleep through most of the meal, snuggled in her carrier.

Annette was commenting on the antiques in the dining room area. Sonja wasn't listening. She was distracted. A man, devouring a plateful of mashed potatoes smothered with beef and gravy, was seated nearby. Sonja recognized him as the man who helped Damon with the granite countertop. *What was his name? How well did he know Damon? Was he a good friend?* Fear gripped her heart.

Sonja wanted to leave, but doing so would mean passing directly in front of the table where the man was sitting. Instinctively, she reached for the baby carrier. If only she could move Grace out of sight. Or perhaps her mother could carry Grace out, and the man would think the child belonged to her. Her mind was racing. She had to protect Grace at all costs.

"Who had the meatloaf?" a voice asked. Sonja looked up to see the server, an older woman, standing just to her left, two plates of food in her hands.

"Oh, that's mine." Annette reached for the plate of food.

"Then you must be the chicken," the server said to Sonja, placing the plate in front of her. Chicken was right. She was so afraid the man to her right would recognize her. She hoped he was too engrossed in his own food to notice.

"Oh, what a cute baby! Yours?" the server asked loudly, looking directly at Sonja. Sonja noticed the man was looking at her, too.

Sonja had little to say as she ate. She could feel the man's eyes on her. Then suddenly, she heard the scraping of his chair on the wood floor. She could feel him coming closer.

"I know you. You're the little lady from the coffeehouse up in Fish Creek."

Sonja had to look up. She couldn't speak. She tried to look confused. Maybe he would think he had the wrong person.

"You know where that boyfriend of yours is hiding out? He owes me."

"I . . . I . . . he owes you?" Sonja stammered. "For the counter?"

"No, he won that, even though I think he cheated. Still owes me four hundred bucks, though."

"What for?" Her mind was racing. *Damon won the countertop? Did this man say Damon cheated? Yeah, well, she could believe that.* She had to think. She had to choose her words carefully. "Damon left some time ago. He doesn't work for me anymore."

The man stepped back. "Oh, sorry. I thought that was his place. He said he was buyin' into it. Well, you're lucky to have gotten rid of him. He was nothin' but a liar and a cheat. And a lousy poker player to boot." With that, the man turned and left.

Annette, who had been quiet through the entire discourse, closed her hand over Sonja's. "You okay, honey?"

Sonja nodded. She was shaking. Damon, the father of her child, was being described as a liar and a cheat. How could she have been so blind? She took a deep breath and closed her eyes. Annette must have thought she was praying. She sat quietly, holding her daughter's hand for a moment.

"Precious Father in Heaven . . . "

Sonja opened her eyes as her mother began praying out loud. "We know You want only what is best for us . . . "

My mom is a true believer. She really thinks God wants the best for me. There was a time when I believed that, too. But now? How could You love me now, God?

"Right now, my little girl is hurting and scared. Please give her comfort and peace . . . "

Comfort? Peace? Haven't I ignored You for these past several years? Didn't I pretend to be a Christian? Faking it has to be a big no-no, right?

"Please protect her and my precious little granddaughter from the evil people in this world . . . "

Evil people. Like Damon. And me. And that was the biggie. Sex outside of marriage. God surely would not be happy over that.

"In the name of Jesus, I ask this. Amen."

Sonja had gone to a teen session with her youth group from church about purity. She made a vow, along with her friends, to remain pure until she married. Yes, God had plenty to hold against her. Yet Sonja was hopeful God would have mercy on her daughter. Grace had done nothing to deserve His anger. As her mother finished praying, Sonja clenched her jaw to stop her chin from quivering. "Yes, please protect Grace, Lord. Amen."

Annette brightened, as if praying had made everything right in her world again. They finished their meal and made their way along the last leg of the trip.

Craig Linder had kindly gone to the shop to turn on the water and get everything ready, so Sonja was not surprised to find one of Joan's famous casseroles waiting for them. Annette set up the portable crib, while Sonja nursed the baby. While the infant slept in her new room, Sonja and Annette unpacked.

She and her mother had baked twenty-four dozen breakfast cookies before leaving Kenosha. Her coffee supplies, including her roasted beans, had been ordered and delivered under the watchful eye of her friend, Rose, who, while waiting for the order to arrive, had cleaned the nursery and hung a picture to welcome the new baby. The picture was a print she found in a store in Sturgeon Bay. It was a little girl sitting in a rocking chair reading a story to her stuffed teddy bear. Joan Linder had put a bouquet of pink silk baby roses on the chest of drawers and lined each drawer with pink paper. Sonja was overwhelmed by their thoughtfulness.

Daniel arrived Saturday night to bring his wife home.

"I hate leaving you," Annette cried as she held her daughter. "I promise I will be back as soon as school is out."

Daniel kissed his granddaughter and hugged Sonja. "I have to admit that caramel macchiato you made me was pretty good. I may never go back to plain old coffee."

"Thanks for being my guinea pig, Dad." She was not drinking anything with caffeine while nursing Grace, so she relied on her parents to try out the products her new espresso machine afforded her. She considered emailing Cindy to tell her how much she appreciated the experience she gained at the Rocky Mountain Coffee Bar, but she was afraid to start up a conversation, even online. She didn't want to give Cindy the opportunity to deliver some "I told you so" speech.

Sonja waved goodbye as the two older Parkers climbed into the car. She put up what she thought was a good front, assuring her mother and father that she and the baby would be fine. Inside, she was secretly willing them to insist they stay, or better yet, insist she and Grace get back in the car with them to go home. But before she knew it, she and Grace were alone.

CHAPTER 24

THE BABY WAS STILL IN the middle of her afternoon nap. Sonja looked at the clock and decided if Grace held true to form, she would have enough time to call the bakery and check her website. By the time she finished, Grace was wide awake, lying on her back, looking up at the mobile hanging above her. Every once in a while, she would shake her little fists and open her mouth as if she had something to say, but no sounds came out. Sonja enjoyed watching her daughter.

She was about to pick Grace up to snuggle her before changing her diaper and feeding her when she heard a loud knock at the door. It couldn't be a customer. The sign on the door clearly stated the coffee shop was closed. Sonja peeked around the corner of the front window and let out a little gasp.

"Mrs. Atchinson! How good to see you."

"Come to see the baby. Well, aren't you going to invite me in?"

Sonja opened the door a bit wider and waved her arm toward the dining area. "Of course. Please."

Mrs. Atchinson shuffled her aging frame through the door and into the dining area. Sonja noted the woman looked even older up close than she had imagined. Her face was lined with wrinkles, and her hands were covered with the brown spots of the aged. She steadied herself with a beautifully carved cane she held in her right hand. In her left, she carried a plastic grocery bag.

Sonja went into the kitchen and retrieved Grace from her play yard. She grabbed a bag of breakfast cookies as well. By the time she returned, Mrs. Atchinson had seated herself at the table near the window.

"Mrs. Atchinson, this is Grace." She sat down in the chair next to the old woman, hoping her frail and elderly neighbor wouldn't ask to hold her daughter. "And I brought us out some cookies."

Mrs. Atchinson was looking Grace over. She put her finger next to Grace's tiny hand. Grace rolled her fingers around the crooked finger tightly.

"There! You see! She's a smart one! And healthy, too. Sickly children don't grab your finger like that." She put the plastic grocery bag on the table. "Here, I made this for her."

"That was very kind of you." Sonja reached in the bag and pulled out a soft, yellow, crocheted baby afghan. "Oh, Mrs. Atchinson, it's beautiful! Thank you!"

"Woulda' made it pink if I'd known it was gonna be a girl," the older woman told her. "Took me more than six months to make. My hands don't work so good anymore."

"Six months? But how did you know?" Sonja's mind was racing. When had she told Joan? That was the only way Mrs. Atchinson could have learned about the baby.

"Nobody told me, if that's what you're thinking," Mrs. Atchinson told her as if reading her mind. "I just knew, that's all. Sometimes, I just know stuff. Like I know she's gonna be a good one. And I know everything is gonna be okay for you now. Now that that one on the motorbike is gone. 'Course, you'll be needing someone to help you out."

There was a part of her that wanted to tell the old woman to mind her own business. Sonja quickly dismissed the thought. Mrs. Atchinson was offering care and support. She had known about the baby. How she knew didn't matter. She knew. She knew, and she didn't shun Sonja as expected. Instead, she had spent grueling hours crocheting a blanket for the baby.

"Had six children myself. Only four lived, though. Had twins. They died right off. We didn't have all the new stuff you have. No doctor, just a midwife. Raised the rest of them in that house over there. Only two left. The girl lives in California and the boy? Well, he run off and married some little girl from Chicago. They come up every Christmas, though. And sometimes in the summer."

"So, do you have any grandchildren?" Sonja had never seen anyone visit the little white house with the picket fence.

"Oh, sure. I got me a whole passel of grands. I got three great-grandchildren, too. You come over sometime, and I'll show you their pictures."

"I'd like that."

Mrs. Atchinson cooed and talked sweetly to Baby Grace for a few more minutes before pushing herself up from the chair and leaning briefly on the table. Sonja handed her the bag of cookies and walked her neighbor to the door, cradling Grace in her arms.

"Mrs. Atchinson," Sonja began tentatively, "I was wondering if someday you might tell me more about Libby and Joe."

A sad smile crept across the old woman's face. "Two of the finest people on earth," she said. "Sure, one day I'll tell you all about them." With that, she made her way across the porch, down the steps, and headed down the walkway toward her own home. Sonja wondered if she should have offered to drive her back. Instead, she watched until Mrs. Atchinson had made it to her gate. By then, Grace was beginning to squirm and cry. She changed the baby's diaper and rested in a chair in her living quarters to nurse the little one before fixing herself something to eat.

"I may not be able to keep this nursing business up when I open the store," Sonja whispered to her daughter. "We'll see." Mrs. Atchinson was right. Sonja needed help to run the shop or help with the baby. Or both.

Sonja hired Joan to help her for two hours a day. Her friend warned her she would be able to do that only until the second week of June. Once Cassie graduated, she was taking her on a trip back East for two weeks. Then she would be driving one of the boys to camp and working at the church camp with her boys in tow for the last week of July.

Sonja put the word out that she would be needing help and even posted it on her website, but to date, had little interest. What she offered was only a part-time job. Hardly enough for someone to live on for the summer. Her best chance at finding someone was at the high school, she decided. As she sat there rocking the baby, she made a plan to ask Cassie if there was a school newspaper or a bulletin board where she might post the job description.

Over the next few weeks Sonja came to appreciate all her own parents had done for her and for Grace. Spending most of her day working in the coffee shop and trying to keep up with mundane chores such as laundry, cooking, and cleaning in the evening left her little time to rest.

Grace seemed to have her days and nights mixed up. She would sleep for long periods of time during the day but be so active and fussy around three in the morning, she couldn't go back to sleep. Neither could Sonja. Losing sleep began to take its toll on the young mother.

The local customers, many of whom Sonja now knew by name, were happy to discover Libby's was once again open for business. Sonja was thrilled to see the response to her offering of specialty coffees, even though her standard "Cuppa Joe" remained her best seller. Joan came every day around eleven o'clock and stayed until one. As long as Grace continued to nurse around 11:30 every day, then go down for a nap, the day schedule was perfect. Joan could handle the lunch crowd that seemed to grow as the weather improved.

Joan wasn't opposed to helping prepare the food or making the regular coffee or tea but lacked confidence to make the iced coffees and specialty drinks now on Libby's chalkboard menu. Sonja tried to teach her a few basics. She showed her the notebook of recipes she had created to remind her of what to do.

"Are you kidding? I'll mess it up," Joan said.

Essential to brewing the espresso properly is making sure the roasted beans had been finely ground. The grinder had different settings. In her sleep-deprived state, Sonja had, on more than one occasion, set the grinder for regular coffee, then tried to make espresso with it. The outcome was a weaker, less flavorful brew. It was a waste of both time and money.

Rose stopped by two or three evenings each week to visit after the library closed. "Grace is so beautiful," Rose said. "She's so cuddly and soft."

"You say that now," Sonja said. "But the minute she cries, I notice you change your tune!"

"I can't help it. I don't know what to do when she cries."

"It's okay. I just appreciate you coming over. It's good to have someone to talk to who can actually talk back."

"If you want backtalk, just wait a few years. I think that comes around thirteen or so."

Sonja laughed. "I guess I did give my mom a rough time back then. But not my dad. I never talked back to my dad."

"Same here. I wonder why that is."

"The only problem Grace gives me is her sleeping pattern. I've read everything I can and tried all kinds of things to get her to sleep at night. She obviously didn't read the same information."

"Maybe as she grows, she'll just change. I think my nephew was like that."

"Maybe. In a few weeks, school's out, and my mom is coming to help. I can hold on until then." *I hope.*

CHAPTER 25

"SWEETHEART, I AM SO SORRY. Are you sure you will be alright?" Annette coughed.

"Of course, Mom. You just get well," Sonja answered. "Grace and I are fine."

The flu. Sonja looked at the phone as she set it back on the desk. Cassie and Joan were on their way to meet Joan's sister and niece in New York City before making their trek together down the coast to South Carolina. There had been no response to her advertisement. Sonja hadn't been too worried, since her mother was planning to help her until the Fourth of July crowd had dispersed. Now this.

Sonja didn't particularly want her mom around if she was sick, but she was in dire need of help. Rose had a full-time job with the library. Mrs. Atchinson, well, that was not an option. Patty Elston, the wife of the glass artist across the street, had a toddler and was now expecting a second child. Sonja would not ask her. The Browns, owners of Sweet Treats, had their own candy store to run. It took both of them working together full-time. She had met a few other locals the couple of times she had been to church and a few who came into the shop from time-to-time, but no one stood out as a likely candidate.

A poster Cassie put up at the high school yielded only a couple of calls, but no one who wanted to work the schedule Sonja suggested for the small amount of money she could offer. With a sigh, Sonja put a "help wanted" sign in the window of the shop. She wasn't hopeful. Sonja began making plans to run everything on her own.

For the first time in a long time, Grace slept a full six hours, from eleven at night until five in the morning. "I should have told you I needed your help sooner," Sonja told her infant daughter. The timing was perfect. Sonja fed the baby and settled her into the infant swing. She put two batches of muffins in the oven before the first customers arrived. The regular coffee was brewing, and the aroma filled the coffee shop.

Her first customers were two women from Green Bay. The younger of the two ordered a caramel macchiato, while the older waited patiently for a latte. Sonja listened to their chatter. Door County was "charming." Fish Creek was "quaint." Libby's Cuppa Joe was "a treasure."

"Are you really looking for help?" the older woman asked Sonja.

"Yes, I am."

"My niece may be interested. I'll have to tell her."

Sonja handed the woman one of her business cards. "Here, she can contact me through this website." She put on her sweetest smile, though she doubted anything would come of it.

Sonja managed to make chicken salad for lunch and pulled two versions of breakfast cookies out of the freezer for her afternoon guests. Plain and butterscotch. The day was warm and busy. Finally, Sonja closed the shop with a sign she created on her computer, stating the new business hours were from 8:00 a.m. to 2:30 p.m. each day. Now if Grace would be so good as to comply with the proposed schedule, she could manage for a few weeks until her mother arrived or until she could hire someone.

Grace didn't get the memo. As good as she had slept the night before, she made up for it by sleeping in only fitful spurts the next. She fussed and cried, then nursed hungrily for a few moments, only to fall asleep in Sonja's arms. When the young mother tried to lay the infant down in the crib Daniel had set up in her room, Grace would wake up about the same time Sonja's head hit the pillow.

"Do you have a sound machine?" Gina asked when Sonja called her the next evening. Gina had been helpful when Sonja was pregnant. She offered her advice on eating and exercise. Now, Sonja called to see what insights she might have about helping Grace develop a good sleep routine.

"Yes, I have a sound machine, and I've tried every setting on it. She seems to like static from the radio the best. But that's when we're in the car."

"Well, of course every baby is different, but my first one was pretty fussy. In fact, we used to put him in the baby carrier and set it on the washer or dryer while it was running to soothe him. You might try giving her a warm bath at the same time each night," Gina offered.

Sonja was grateful for the help but especially grateful that Gina didn't treat her like an incompetent mother. In fact, Gina encouraged Sonja and assured her the time of sleepless nights would pass.

But when? Will I ever get another full night of sleep?

She had a deal with the bakery. Every Friday, she would call to confirm her order for the next week, and they delivered the fresh-baked bread and croissants each morning. On Friday, she forgot to call. She forgot to call Saturday. They weren't open on Sunday; and on Monday, her sandwiches were served on the plain, store-bought white bread she coaxed Rose into buying on her way to open the library that morning.

Then there was the fiasco with the muffins. She had purchased self-rising flour instead of regular flour, so her muffins tasted dry and salty. She threw the entire batch away and had started mixing a new batch before she discovered the mistake. Now, she had wasted a half-dozen eggs and some cooking oil as well. She pulled a box of muffin mix from her resident kitchen to see her through the morning, then proceeded to forget to set the timer. The smoke alarm sounded just as she was serving coffee to a busload of senior citizens touring the county. Although she assured them it was not a fire, they scurried like mice to flee the building, leaving cups of coffee and remnants of cookies everywhere.

Sonja turned off the oven and turned on the fan. She opened a window and sat down in the middle of the kitchen to join Grace in having a good cry.

"Hello?" came the youthful voice from the dining area. Sonja straightened herself up and resigned herself to tell whomever had come in that the store was closed.

A young woman peeked around the corner into the kitchen. "Hi there. Are you Sonja Parker? I'm here about the job."

Melissa Johnson turned out to be a personable young woman. She had just completed her junior year at a small Christian college in the Midwest and had come home to Green Bay for the summer. Her aunt had visited Door County the previous week and told her of the job opening.

She hated to tell the girl it was only a part-time job. She had driven all the way from Green Bay. Instead, she offered Melissa a cup of coffee and explained she needed an experienced coffee barista.

"But I am experienced. I am the senior barista at the campus coffeehouse." Melissa handed Sonja an envelope.

Sonja set the envelope on the counter by the phone. She knew she should tell the girl this was only a part-time position. Maybe only a couple of hours a day. But something inside her told her to offer a position to the woman before her. Suddenly, an idea came to mind.

"It doesn't pay much, but room and board are included. I have a baby and need someone to help with the shop, so I can take care of her. You'd be sharing the apartment with us."

"With your whole family?" Melissa asked tentatively.

"It's just the two of us. Me and my daughter, Grace." As if on cue, Grace cried from her play yard set up on the closed-in utility porch. Sonja retrieved the child and introduced her to Melissa.

Sonja invited Melissa in to see the kitchen and take a look at the apartment downstairs. Her mind was racing, trying to remember in what condition she had left the apartment. The whole morning was a blur.

The fan in the kitchen was still whirring wildly. The burnt muffins were resting on the top of the stove, still welded to the muffin tin with a black, sugary goo that had once been blueberries. Sonja started to explain. The bell above the door sounded, and a group of locals made their way into the dining room. Melissa immediately began cleaning up the mess. Sonja put Grace in her swing and took orders for coffee, taking complimentary cookies out to her customers.

A few minutes later, a group of tourists made their way up the walkway. Melissa reported a coffee cake with streusel topping would be ready in minutes. The smell of cinnamon filled the air, once again inviting guests to sit down, relax, and wait for a piece of the warm breakfast cake. Sonja took the orders, and soon, she and Melissa were working in tandem, making a variety of coffees and teas for the visitors.

"Okay, it looks like you're already working for Libby's." Sonja grabbed a sleeve of disposable cups from the cupboard.

"I love this place," Melissa responded. "It's exactly what I need." The store had closed, and the kitchen had been cleaned before Melissa ever had a chance to check out the apartment.

Sonja did a quick pick-up of the folded laundry resting on the back of the couch. There were a couple of dishes in the sink and the cereal box still on the table, but then, everything didn't have to be perfect. She told Melissa she could have her choice of rooms. She and Grace would share a space.

"This is incredibly perfect," Melissa assured her. "I have two online classes to complete this summer if I hope to do my student teaching in the fall semester."

"Oh, you want to be a teacher? My mom teaches third grade in Kenosha."

"Really?" Melissa sounded excited. "My grandparents live in Racine. I'm hoping to maybe get a teaching job in Wisconsin eventually. There's just something about being close to family."

Sonja liked this girl. "So, where did you learn how to bake? At home? Or did you do that at the coffeehouse at your college?"

"At home. We serve great stuff at school, but the cook in the cafeteria bakes everything and just sends it across campus to the coffeehouse."

"So, do you want the job?" Sonja asked pointedly.

"I think so. I'll go home and pray about it and let you know in the morning. I'll call early if I decide not to take it and arrive early if I decide to work and live here. How's that?"

"Sounds great."

Melissa left. Sonja fed Grace and gave her a bath before putting her down to sleep. She sang a soft lullaby to her, whispered words of love and affection in the baby's ear, and laid her down in her crib. She had already tiptoed out of the room when she remembered the sound machine. Should she go back? See what happened? Forget the machine and try to not make any startling noises? She didn't want to open the door and risk waking the sleeping babe.

Finally, Sonja retrieved an old radio stored on the utility porch. She plugged it in the hall outlet; and once she located static, she turned the volume up and put it just outside the baby's bedroom door.

It was only as Sonja lay in her own bed that night that she started to question her impetuous offer to Melissa. *I don't really know this girl. I should have asked for references. What if she's some kind of crazy person? No, she wasn't crazy. She was nice. Still, the prudent thing to do would have been to check her out before offering her a job.* Actually, it wasn't offering her the job that was the problem, Sonja admitted to herself. It was offering to open her home up to someone she didn't know at all. "What was I thinking?"

CHAPTER 26

A RASH DECISION. **SONJA COULDN'T** sleep. Something was nagging at her—something she should remember—something just out of reach.

The envelope. Melissa had handed her an envelope when they first met. What was in it? What had she done with it? Sonja crept upstairs to the work kitchen and replayed the morning. She walked toward the doorway. There, in the shadows, lay the envelope next to the telephone.

She opened it. A resumé. That was good. A copy of a background check for student teaching—excellent. Melissa's transcript. Not bad. In fact, her grades were better than Sonja's had been. And a letter.

Sonja read the letter of recommendation from Melissa's supervisor at the university's coffeehouse. Melissa was described as personable. *True.* She was described as hard-working and a person who would take initiative. *I certainly witnessed that myself.* And she was described as a godly woman. *Hmm, yes, even Melissa's comment that she would have to pray about the job demonstrated her faith. Well, as long as she doesn't try to shove her religion on me.*

Two weeks later, soft strains of music filled the dining area. Melissa was proving to be more helpful than Sonja ever imagined. She "donated" her sound system to Libby's. Through it, she played a collection of instrumentals for the customers. Sonja recognized familiar tunes from time-to-time. Customers, mostly locals, made positive comments about the music.

Another talent Melissa shared with her new employer was how to make kringle. Sonja had eaten the flaky Danish pastry many times. It was a specialty of the Racine area, the name of both the county and the town north of Kenosha.

Melissa's maternal grandmother in Racine was Danish and had taught the girl how to make it. To acquire the flaky layers of dough required at least three days of preparation. Melissa taught Sonja how to make the traditional pastry with its almond paste filling but happily created the oval-shaped Danish pastries with fruit fillings as well. Sonja's favorite was the cherry, followed closely by the apple cinnamon one Melissa made for the customers of Libby's.

"I don't know how I managed without her," Sonja told Fran over the phone one evening. "But she does have this private side . . . "

"Private side?"

"Well, she spends a lot of time holed up in her room, working on her online courses; and every Sunday, she goes off to some traveling church."

"What's a traveling church? She's not in some cult or something, is she?"

"No, I think it's just a small group, so they meet in houses."

"Be careful. Some of those zealots are scary."

Sonja laughed. Nothing about Melissa was scary. In fact, Melissa encouraged Sonja and embraced new ideas for Libby's.

* * *

"Let's do it," Melissa said when Sonja told her about her idea to have book talks in the upper room. "I'll help."

A few clicks on the computer, and Melissa had tracked down three authors in Door County who might come for a local author series. She also suggested they could invite the authors of a book called *A Door County Christmas* to come during the week of the pumpkin festival.

The two decided to read some of these books before they moved forward on anything. The next day, Melissa made a trip to the library and secured copies of eight books published by local authors and three books featuring Door County as the setting. Sonja could see there was no turning back. No procrastinating. Melissa was willing to help, so the two of them divided the titles and began reading.

"I'd like to get Mavis Harmon as our first guest author," Sonja said after the store closed the next day. "She wrote a historical account of the peninsula, peppered with local recipes. And guess what one of those recipes is . . . kringle! According to the story, one of the prominent citizens of the area found his wife in Racine, Wisconsin. She won his heart by baking kringle and shared the recipe with Mrs. Harmon when she moved to Bailey's Harbor."

"Yes! And I could make kringle for the event!"

"The only problem is that Mrs. Harmon's book is out of print."

"We'll print up copies of the kringle recipe to distribute. I think everyone would love to hear the history; and that way, they'll have something to take home."

"Rose says Mrs. Harmon is still a vibrant and well-respected member of the community. I think I'll call her."

When Sonja finally tracked down her number, Mrs. Harmon said she was always happy to talk "with anyone anytime about Door County." Sonja scheduled a meeting on Wednesday afternoon to discuss the book reading to be offered at Libby's.

The idea was exciting. When Grace was born, Sonja had essentially put everything on hold. She was happy to just keep the store running, willing to forfeit her dreams of reestablishing Libby's Cuppa Joe as a popular attraction in Fish Creek. Now, she had an espresso machine, an experienced barista, kringle added to the menu, and the possibility of an author visit.

She left Melissa in charge of emailing Cynthia Ruchti, one of the four authors of *A Door County Christmas.* A bit of research revealed the noted writer and speaker lived in Wisconsin.

Melissa pecked away at her computer. "I'll see if she's available to come sometime in October."

"The budget is tight this year, and it would be extremely short notice. Ask if she can do it next year. Find out how much she charges."

"About the room upstairs," Melissa began, "I know you want to host the author visits and maybe get in some musicians. I have another idea that would bring in a little money every week."

"Every week? What did you have in mind?"

"Part of the reason I wanted to come to Door County was because of a small church plant here."

"A church plant?"

"It's a new church starting up."

"I understand. I just didn't realize that was part of the draw. I thought you came because of the great impression I made that first day we met." Sonja winked. "So, how many people are in this church?"

"We usually have about fifteen or sixteen, but we're growing. Right now, we meet in people's houses. We're growing, and soon, that won't work. We meet from nine o'clock to 10:30, and the shop doesn't open until noon on Sundays, so . . . "

"I hadn't thought about renting the space weekly. Can I tell you tomorrow?"

"Sure!"

"There is one thing, though. And this is a problem I need to solve, anyway. I have only about ten folding chairs upstairs in the storage closet. I figure I need to get at least ten to fifteen more to host the author groups up there."

"Kevin—he's the pastor of the church—has some chairs. He's been bringing them to the houses in his truck. I don't know how many, but I'm sure he'll loan you the chairs. Do you want me to ask him?"

"Let's wait until we decide about the church meeting here and see if we actually get an author visit going, okay?"

"Okay." Melissa was quiet, but Sonja knew when she got an idea, she was like a puppy with a new tennis shoe.

* * *

Mavis Harmon lived in a small cottage in Bailey's Harbor on the other side of the peninsula. Sonja had visited the small town earlier with Damon.

Mrs. Harmon stood on the porch as Sonja closed the car door. "Hope you didn't have any trouble finding it."

"No problem at all. I just put your address in my GPS."

"Your what? Oh, that thing for the car?"

Sonja looked around the tiny yard. "Your flowers are beautiful."

"Thank you. Don't do so much anymore. My son, Jack, comes over and messes with it. He lives a couple miles down the road. Come on in."

Sonja followed the woman into the house. The living room was large. Antique furniture lined the walls. A beautiful rolltop desk was cluttered with papers and books. An upholstered couch, similar to the one the Davises had left behind, was covered with clear vinyl.

At Mrs. Harmon's beckoning, Sonja sat down in a dark red, velvet, overstuffed chair.

"Thank you so much for seeing me, Mrs. Harmon."

"Just Mavis. You don't need to call me Mrs. Harmon."

"Okay, Mavis. Thank you. As I mentioned on the phone, I wanted to talk to you about doing an author talk at Libby's Cuppa Joe in Fish Creek."

"Yes, but folks can't get my book anymore."

"I know, but we would advertise it as you sharing a bit of Door County history. You could share a few good stories. We think the tourists would love it, and we'll try to get locals there as well."

"So, how long are you thinking?"

"Well, we thought you could share, answer some questions, and then we could have a small reception. Maybe an hour for the whole thing? Some people might stay behind and want to talk with you more if you would want to do that." Sonja studied Mrs. Harmon's face. *Was she frowning?* "Of course, we're flexible."

"I could probably do that. Jack could bring me. But I can't manage climbing stairs, you know. A few steps, like up to the porch, is okay, though. Jack will help me."

This put a new wrinkle in the plan. The whole idea was to make use of the upper room. *No turning back now. We could possibly do it one evening or on a Wednesday afternoon like today when business was typically slow. Maybe take reservations to assure a good turnout.*

"Don't worry. We'll work it out. And my assistant, Melissa, had a great idea for the reception. She thought she would make the traditional kringle you wrote about in your book for the reception. How does that sound?"

Mavis Harmon clapped her hands together in delight. "Kringle! Oh, it has been years since I tasted homemade kringle."

"We thought we could give everyone a copy of the recipe and maybe share the story you had in the book about the woman who moved to Bailey's Harbor when she married and taught you how to make kringle."

"And maybe she'll come, too."

"Who will come?"

"Margaret. She could come to the talk. I think she would like that you're serving her kringle."

"The woman in the book? She's still around?"

"Oh, sure. After her husband, Judson, died, she married Eli Atchinson. Lives there in Fish Creek real close to the coffee shop."

"Margaret Atchinson? She lives across the street."

"She's the one that taught me and Libby how to make kringle. I haven't seen her since Libby's funeral."

Why, of course the Harmons and Davises knew each other. Both had lived all their lives on the peninsula.

"So, Libby made kringle for the coffee shop?"

"Oh, sure. She was a fine hand at it. Didn't make it after the accident, though."

"What accident?"

"Why, when their boy, Joey, died," Mavis said with a tone that told Sonja she should already know that. But how could she? She hadn't known the Davises at all. "It's in the book."

Mavis' book. Of course.

"I guess I need to read more carefully and not just study the recipes," she offered by way of an apology.

Mavis laughed. "When is this shindig I'm supposed to talk at anyway?"

"Well, I was thinking we could maybe set it up during this year's pumpkin festival."

"October? Won't be here. I always spend September with my sister, and then we head to Florida for the winter. I'll do it in August. You got a calendar?"

Sonja fished in her purse. "August is coming soon. I'll need time to get posters out and everything."

Sonja hadn't even figured out which day might work. She needed time. August? August seemed to be much too soon. Then again, maybe if she could get something in the weekly and if she could print flyers to post at the condos in the area, then just maybe she could pull this off. It was her first attempt. Mavis was doing it for free. *This may be a good time to try the idea out.* Tourists would still be around through the second week of August. Then school would be starting, and the numbers would thin. People were always looking for something different to do mid-week. Sonja made a quick decision.

"How about Wednesday, August eighth? We can do it in the evening and serve the kringle as a dessert."

"Let me check my social calendar." Mavis flashed a grin and gave a wave of her hand. "Yes, I believe I am available that evening. I will pencil you in."

"Maybe we should make sure your son is available to drive you."

"You're right, of course." Mavis pushed herself up from her chair and walked over to a small, round table in the corner of the room. There, she picked up her telephone and called Jack, who in turn confirmed he would drive her to Libby's Cuppa Joe on August eighth. They spoke for a few minutes more, the conversation peppered with "kringle" and "Margaret" and ending with an "I'll ask" before Mavis returned.

"He asked if you're going to have breakfast cookies, too. Apparently, he stops by your place frequently and says the butterscotch ones are his favorites."

"I'll be sure to have some just for him."

When she returned to Libby's, Grace was resting peacefully in her crib. Sonja and Melissa set about immediately drafting a colorful flyer to hang around town and to distribute to the condominium complexes and bed and breakfasts that housed the county's tourists. They decided to write a brief biography of Mavis Harmon with an invitation for the event to be placed in the weekly. They had three weeks to put this together and get a group of interested people to attend. And first on their list was Margaret Atchinson.

That evening, Sonja began a careful reading of Mavis Harmon's book, resisting the urge to just flip through the pages searching for the names of people she knew. Maybe in these pages, she would find the answers to her questions about Libby and Joe Davis.

CHAPTER 27

"**THE UPPER ROOM IS THE** largest area," Sonja said as they made their way up the open stairway. She couldn't believe the pastor of Melissa's church was the same man she thought to be a rough, unfriendly farmer.

The large room was twice the size of the dining room below it, covering the dining area and kitchen.

"I don't have a lot of chairs. You'd need to bring some." Sonja opened the door to the storage area. "There's a table in here and a small bookcase you could use, if you like."

Kevin Hanson walked to the large window in the front. The lake was clearly visible. "The Upper Room. Sounds like the perfect place for a group of Christ-followers to gather, eh?"

Sonja had always called the space "the upper room" but had not made a biblical connection until now. "The Upper Room," she repeated, remembering stories she had learned as a child of the last meal Jesus had shared with His disciples.

The two settled on a price, which included coffee. Kevin explained that the invoice would be paid by the team sponsoring the young church plant. That had been a week ago. Now Sonja, Grace, Daniel, and Annette sat with the regular attenders of Kevin's church.

Annette and Daniel Parker beamed as one by one the group of believers spoke to them at the coffee table. Sonja knew the main source of their joy was the infant granddaughter Annette held in her arms.

She also suspected, though, they were excited about the prospect of a church meeting in the coffee shop. And although she attended the service out of curiosity, Sonja had to admit she had enjoyed herself.

Kevin Hanson was not like the preacher she had grown up hearing speak each Sunday from behind a tall, wooden pulpit. He didn't wear a suit or tie, and he was very transparent about his own inadequacies. At first, Sonja thought her parents might be offended by the casualness of the service. Instead, they were interested in the roots of the church and its mission.

"So, how long were you in Ecuador?" Daniel asked Kevin after the service.

"Almost two years. I was already leaving at the end of the month, anyway, when my dad had his first heart attack and my mother needed me here."

"So, you started the church," Annette said.

"Well, not right away. Actually, I was a bit resistant to starting a church here, but God had a different idea."

Sonja couldn't stay to listen to the rest. She needed to check the air pot and make sure the creamer and sugar was available.

"He's a nice young man," Daniel said later.

Annette wrapped a tray of breakfast cookies in foil. "I think so, too. I like him."

"I guess," Sonja said. "But the first time I met him, I thought he was rude."

"He told me about his first visit to the coffee shop," Daniel said. "I think he knows he didn't make such a good impression."

"Really?" Sonja ran hot water through the air pot.

"Yeah, well, it seems he had worked all morning on his father's farm after being up half the night helping birth a calf. He came into town to purchase some supplies and stopped by the coffee shop. He didn't even get to finish eating his muffin when he got a call that his father had been rushed to the hospital with another heart attack."

That explains a lot. "So, what was that about Ecuador?" Sonja asked, trying to not sound too interested.

"He worked in Ecuador as a missionary. When his dad had his first heart surgery, he came home. Kevin's younger brother was in the middle of his tour of duty in Afghanistan, so his mother asked him to stay."

"And he just decided to start up a church?"

"I don't think it works quite like that," Daniel said. "The way he explained it, one of his seminary professors contacted him because a church planting organization was interested in supporting a church plant in Door County. He asked Kevin to write up what he thought a new church could bring to the area. They named it Open Door Ministries. I guess it was to capitalize on the Door County name, but it's kind of funny because the coffee shop is as close as they've ever been to having a regular meeting place with any kind of door, open or not."

I wonder what he could possibly have written to gain their support. There are several churches in the area already. Okay, it is more casual than other churches. The music was different, too, led by a Puerto Rican named Diego playing softly on a classical guitar. But surely, there was something else. Something more to this group. She decided she would ask Melissa about it later. Her parents were leaving in the morning, and she didn't want to spend the rest of her time with them talking about church.

The coffee shop customers thinned in the late afternoon, so Sonja closed up, packed a light snack, and walked with her parents to Peninsula State Park, Grace snuggled in the baby pack strapped to her. The longer days of summer allowed for a leisurely walk along the trails that wove through the woods and dipped down to the water's edge. Soon, Grace was asleep in the baby carrier, and the three adults silently embraced the beauty of the park. The occasional sound of a bird chirping or the water lapping against the rocks was interrupted only by the laughter of children playing in the sand or the bicyclists humming along the bike trails.

"Hasn't this been a perfect day?" Annette asked.

It has been a wonderful day. Her mother may be talking about the weather, but something told Sonja that agreeing to having Kevin's church meet in the "Upper Room" would be a welcome addition to Libby's Cuppa Joe. The extra income helped, but there was something more. Community. That was it. Having the church meet there made Sonja—and Libby's—more a part of the community. That had to be good for business.

Melissa's description of the church's mission later that evening affirmed Sonja's decision. As the young woman described it, there were several churches already established in the county; but while they were sharing the Word, it was mostly with people who came to them.

"My dad describes the thought process for many well-established churches as the 'if you build it, they will come' mentality. He doesn't mean anything bad by it. Those churches are doing a great work. He just knows there are a lot of people who will never step foot in a church building. My dad's a minister in Green Bay. This new church is all about serving people and building lasting relationships. I wanted to be a part of it because it's based on the idea that everyone has the right to hear about Jesus. What they decide to do with that information is up to them. I'll still love them and help them anyway I can. You see, ultimately the decision is theirs and theirs alone. Just like you can't be a Christian just because your parents are, you know what I mean? You make your own decision to believe. And if you truly believe, you follow. It's an individual choice.

"And the other thing is, well, you get to a place like Door County, where life seems pretty good, and people start thinking, 'Hey, I don't have it so bad. Why do I need all that church stuff?' You know, people think they are good and rarely realize they can never be good enough."

Melissa wasn't addressing her personally; but as Sonja lay in bed that night, she couldn't help but think about her young employee's words. *No, I can never be good enough.*

CHAPTER 28

MARGARET ATCHINSON WAS GIDDY WHEN Sonja told her Mavis Harmon agreed to come to the coffee shop to speak.

"She's a dear friend of mine. Known her near as long as I've lived in Door County."

Sonja nodded. "We're going to serve kringle. Mrs. Harmon said Libby used to bake kringle at the coffee shop but stopped after the accident."

"What do you know about that?"

"The accident? Well, only what I read in the book—that Libby and Joe's son, Joey, fell through the ice on the lake and drowned."

Mrs. Atchinson put her cup down and sat back in the chair on the front porch of her little house, where the two sat sipping tea and munching on warm cinnamon twists pastries from Sonja's oven. She closed her eyes. She was so still and quiet, for a moment, Sonja thought the old woman had fallen asleep. When she opened her eyes, Sonja could see they were moist.

"Libby never quite got over the loss of that boy," Mrs. Atchinson whispered.

"How old was he? The book only said he and three other teens took a shortcut home from school, and he fell through the ice."

Mrs. Atchinson wiped her eyes with her napkin. "Joey was sixteen years old. And it wasn't a shortcut exactly. It was his sister, Judy; my girl, Sada; and one of the Granger girls, Ellen. They were coming home, for sure, but went out of their way to go by the lake.

"Joey was sweet on Ellen. Judy and Sada gave him a hard time about it. I guess they were teasing him pretty bad, and, well, he started showing off. He said he could beat them home. They started running and giggling, the way girls will do. They took the path, and Joey said he was going across the inlet on the ice. Judy looked back just as he went under; but of course, there was no getting to him. Took the men two days to get his body. They were lucky to find it at all."

Sonja's hands flew to her mouth. "How awful!"

"It was like a dark cloud came over Fish Creek and just stayed there. Libby and Joe walked around like robots. And Judy? She never got through with blaming herself. Supposed to graduate that year with Sada, but she run off. Libby and Joe lost both their children that year. It was hard."

"So how long was Judy gone?"

Mrs. Atchinson looked down and shook her head slowly. "She never came back. Poor old Libby never gave up hope, though. Never wanted to leave the peninsula, just in case her daughter came home. Only went to Green Bay when she was so sick, poor thing."

"Where did Judy go?" *She must have stayed nearby, or else how would she have learned of her father's illness? She had visited him. Hadn't she?* Actually, as Sonja thought about it, she wasn't at all sure Judy had ever visited Joe. He talked about her, but no one ever confirmed she was around.

" . . . where, I don't know," Mrs. Atchinson was saying. "I don't think they ever knew, and I don't think they ever heard from her again."

Once home, Sonja made a quick check on her sleeping baby. She told Melissa she had to do something in the Upper Room but to call for her if business picked up and her service was needed.

Daniel had removed the larger crates holding the espresso machine and the coffee grinder along with the various parts, but the storage closet was still filled with personal items once belonging to the Davises. Sonja quickly scanned the various boxes until she found the one she wanted. She tugged the box out into the middle of the wood floor of the Upper Room.

School pictures chronicling each grade Judy and Joey had attended at the local school were neatly organized with the child's name and grade written in what Sonja now recognized as Libby's handwriting on the back. An envelope with report cards showed both children to be "bright with good social skills." Several teachers had written notes on the back about what a "sensitive and caring" girl Judy was or describing Joey as an "energetic boy" with a "great sense of humor." Sonja poked through the box of memories carefully preserved by a loving mother. She was looking for a letter, a postcard, something. Anything to reveal that Judy had been in touch in some way.

As she was sifting through the artifacts, a lump formed in her throat, and Sonja's shoulder's quaked. She sat back on her heels on the floor, mourning for Libby. Mourning for her loss. Sonja held in her hands all that was left of the lives of two children now lost and the heartbreak of a mother and father who did nothing but love their son and daughter.

Sorting through the artifacts, Sonja pieced together the lives of the Davis children. Judy was only thirteen months older than her brother. A year in age but two years apart in school. Three newspaper clippings told of the accidental drowning, Joey's smiling school picture in each one. The obituary was short. But then, how much life could be reported for a sixteen-year-old boy? A shabby teddy bear was near the bottom of the box. *A favorite toy of one of the children? Or maybe both?* A cherished memory for Libby and Joe of a better time in their lives. A time lost. Someone had tied a ribbon around a stack of sympathy cards from a community of friends and family sharing their grief. Sonja carefully put it all back in the box. She left the room no closer to discovering the whereabouts of Judy than when she started.

The next week seemed to fly by with a record number of customers in the coffee shop. Sonja and Melissa used what spare time they could manage to distribute the flyers they had created to a number of area resorts and a few local bed and breakfast establishments.

The editor of *The Advocate* promised to place an ad for them in the newspaper, and Rose posted the flyer at the library with one of the two copies of Mavis' book the library owned displayed in a glass case beneath it. Several local shops—including the Elston Glass, Sweet Treats, and the Brown's candy store—displayed the colorful flyer in their storefront windows. Craig Linder agreed to put one in Dewey's Bait and Tackle, even though he and Sonja agreed his clientele was not likely to give the event much consideration. Craig told Sonja his entire family would be home by the end of the following week. He sounded relieved. He said in all likelihood, she could count on Joan and Cassie to attend.

By week's end, six people had called in reservations to hear Mavis Harmon give her talk on the history of the county. All locals. On Thursday, Melissa squealed with delight.

"You're not going to believe this, Sonja," she called as she raced up the steps to what Sonja called the coffee shop kitchen. "Remember when you told me to see if one of the authors of *A Door County Christmas* would be available for the pumpkin festival?"

"Are you going to say one of them will come next year?"

"Well, I don't know about *next* year, but Cynthia Ruchti can come this year!" Melissa giggled.

"This year? This October?" Sonja was shocked.

"She emailed me back and said it sounds like fun. She lives in Wisconsin. She and her husband love Door County; and as it happens, she's not scheduled for anything that week, except for a women's Bible study Tuesday morning. We need to look at the calendar and send her some dates back!" Melissa was fairly dancing around the kitchen, balancing her laptop on one arm and poised to type with the other.

The first two days of August brought with them spurts of rain and a sudden drop in temperature, driving more business into Libby's Cuppa Joe. Sonja and Melissa baked kringle, muffins, and cookies by the dozens. Customers enjoyed sandwiches and coffee or tea throughout the day. Children had the option of juice or hot chocolate, and soon the store was running low on the hot chocolate and lower still on miniature marshmallows to scoop into each cup.

Sonja noticed a number of the members of the growing church were stopping by in the middle of the week to share a cup of the brew. She was beginning to learn their names and surprised to discover she looked forward to their visits. Kevin was becoming a regular as well, often arriving after the early crowd and before the lunch crew started ordering sandwiches or the vegetable soup Sonja had recently placed on the menu.

The Sunday messages were surprisingly interesting. Kevin was not an entertainer. Nor was he a professor. He was simple, direct, and spoke from his heart. Everything he said was backed up with verses from the Bible. And what he said seemed to be consistent with all Melissa had shared regarding the mission of the newly formed church.

"God created you. He gave you the ability to make choices. You—and I'm referring here to all of us—chose to turn away from Him. That is sin. Sin separates you from God. God loves you. His desire is to have a relationship with you. But the only way for that to happen is to get rid of the sin. Tall order." He stopped and took a drink of water, letting the idea sink in to the hearts and minds of his small congregation.

"The simple truth is this—you can't get rid of your sin. You can't restore that relationship by just being a better person. A lot of people think they have to get everything just right before they can even think about having a relationship with God. So, how do you get rid of your sin? You can't. Only God can.

"You see, sin requires a penalty, a fine to be paid. A sacrifice made. It requires a huge sacrifice. A blood sacrifice. But God loves you so much, He made a way for that penalty to be paid for you. It is His gift to you. All you have to do—and this is so simple, in a way, it is hard to believe—but all you have to do is accept the gift. Jesus paid your debt for you. Accept that simple truth. Admit your choices have separated you from God.

"But there is so much more. You see, Jesus paid for your sins with His own death, but He didn't stay dead. He rose up from the grave. Only God is capable of doing that. Of living forever. When you accept His sacrifice, you receive the gift of life. You get to enjoy a forever relationship with God."

Sonja had never heard the message presented so succinctly. So straightforward. So directly aimed at her. She did believe God created her. She did make choices. She was a good person but had to admit some of her choices were wrong. Yes, she chose to turn her back on God. But did God still want a relationship with her? Now? It was hard to imagine.

She found herself wanting to ask Kevin about her situation, but the time was never right. With other customers drifting in and out, the demands of the kitchen, and her own desire to spend every available moment with Grace, the only conversations she and Kevin engaged in were casual at best.

He told her about growing up on the farm in Door County.

She told him about Kenosha.

He told her about his experience at the seminary.

She talked of her college days.

He told her about Ecuador.

She spoke of San Diego.

She had assumed he had always wanted to be a preacher, so she was shocked when one day at the coffee shop, he told her how he came to be a Christian.

CHAPTER 29

"THE MINUTE I GRADUATED FROM high school, I ran away from home," Kevin admitted. "Actually, I didn't so much as stick around for the big ceremony or anything. It didn't matter. I didn't like the way my dad would boss me around. The way he expected me to work his farm as though I didn't have a life of my own."

Sonja was quiet. Kevin took a sip of his coffee. "I got a job in Milwaukee at a small gas station, slash convenience store for a while. Stayed with friends when I didn't have enough money for a room. It was pretty bad."

"Did your parents come after you?" *My parents would be frantic. I'm sure Libby and Joe tried to find Judy.*

"No. My dad was pretty rough on us boys back then. My oldest brother left as soon as he turned sixteen and could drop out of school, and my younger brother joined the army as soon as he was old enough. My dad probably said 'good riddance' or something like that. He was a mean old man back then."

Sonja shuddered. She couldn't imagine her dad ever acting in such a way.

"Eventually, I called my mom and told her I was okay," Kevin continued. "Just fed up. Then I went to Chicago, where I heard I could get a good job."

Sonja sat quietly. She couldn't picture Kevin as the type to run away from home and venture out the way he did. *But if things were that bad . . .*

"I wasn't a Christian then. Oh, I had been to Sunday school and stuff like that on and off through the years, but I never let any of it sink in. It wasn't part of our life at home, really. My mom would drag us to church on Easter and Christmas and sometimes on Mother's Day." He paused and took a deep breath. "When I worked in Chicago, I started drinking with the guys and stuff. Going to bars, getting in fights. It wasn't a very happy life."

"Is that why you came back?"

Kevin took a sip of his coffee. "No. It had to get worse before it got better." He was looking in Sonja's eyes, now. She could see he was about to tell her something important. Something he could trust her to know. His arms on the table, he leaned forward. "Sonja, I killed a man."

The words hung in the air, heavy and dark. A knot formed in her throat. *Did he say he killed someone? Surely, he meant something else.*

Kevin cleared his throat and eased back in his chair. He rubbed his hand over his mouth and pulled at his chin. "It was late one night. A bunch of us were hanging out at some local dive. A football game was on, and some of the guys started arguing over one of the calls a ref made. A fight broke out. I was right in the middle of it. Anyway, I punched one guy a little too hard. He fell back and never got up. Next thing I know, I'm in jail for manslaughter."

If someone had asked, "Who is the last person on earth to harm anyone," Sonja would have said, "Kevin Hanson, of course." Kevin was a strong man—probably from all those years of working on the farm. But he was a gracious and loving man, too. Gentle. Still . . . in a fight? Maybe.

"It sounds like it was an accident."

"Yeah, well, I was in jail, accident or not. I didn't have any money for bail, and I wasn't about to call my folks and tell them what I'd done. After I was arraigned and they were taking me back to my cell, my public defender handed me a Bible. He told me to make good use of my time. That Bible was all I had. So, I read it cover to cover. Twice."

"How long were you there?" Sonja asked in a low voice. A customer had just walked in and was ordering a latté from Melissa.

"Two months. It was a gift really. Two months to dry out. Two months to read and study God's Word. Two incredible months."

"And then?"

"And then I went to trial. I was convicted of manslaughter but released for time served. Sonja, they could have put me away forever, and I would have understood. I was responsible for taking a human life. I knew God had forgiven me. I was just surprised the court saw fit to basically forgive me, too. That's when I decided to serve God with all I have in me. I started by working at a halfway house for men released from prison. I worked my way through seminary there. Then I got an offer to work with a missionary team in Ecuador. They needed someone with farm experience."

"Did your parents ever find out?"

"They know. Everyone knows. The thing about sin is you can never really hide it. I told them everything. I told everyone at church, too. I'm not proud of what I did or the life I was leading. I don't tell people to wow them or anything. I share only because of God's grace. This is my story. Everyone has one. God extends His grace, His forgiveness, and His love to each of us."

"There's one thing, though. I've seen your parents. They come to the church."

Kevin's smile stretched across his face. "Funny how it works, isn't it? My dad wouldn't step foot in a church when I was growing up. He had a strange idea about what church was all about. He thought it was 'a bunch of people always asking for money to do stuff for people who should be out there getting a job.'"

Sonja laughed at Kevin's impersonation of his dad.

"He was mean and hard on us because that's the way his dad was with him. Turns out, he didn't like himself very much, either."

"So, what changed? His heart attack?"

"That got his attention, for sure, but you'll have to ask him to tell you his story someday. It gives you hope for all people out there."

The words stayed with Sonja long after Kevin left the coffee shop. *Everyone has a story. Yeah, I have a story. I've done terrible things. And I don't like myself all that much either. But where does God fit in? I'm not so sure He'd forgive me. I knew what I was doing. What Kevin did was an accident. And he didn't go to church before. I don't have that excuse. Nope, I think somewhere in the Bible it says that if we know better and still do something wrong . . .* "I forget . . ." *What does it say?*

CHAPTER 30

MAVIS HARMON DID NOT DISAPPOINT any of the twenty-three attendees at Libby's first author visit event. She was animated and funny, weaving historical accounts of a strong community with whimsical accounts of pranks locals played on each other. She spent a fair amount of time recounting the history of Libby's Cuppa Joe, painting it as the heart of Fish Creek.

Mavis offered an excerpt from the book to print alongside the kringle recipe distributed. In the end, Sonja and Melissa created a folded program with a picture of Mavis on the front, the recipe and an excerpt from the book inside, and a picture of Libby's Cuppa Joe on the back with the website address. Everyone loved the kringle, and most asked Mavis to autograph their program.

The attendees wanted Margaret Atchinson's autograph as well, since Mavis had introduced her as "the one" to bring kringle to Door County. Sonja doubted she was the first, but she certainly had a place in the county's history. Sonja smiled as several of the tourists, all women, had their picture made with the two aging celebrities.

"I would call that a success!" Sonja said as the last of the guests headed out the door.

"A big success," Rose added. "Wasn't she fun? And Melissa, the kringle was excellent! I had tried only the fruited ones before."

"Yeah, the almond paste is really traditional," Melissa said. "We'll have to read *A Door County Christmas* carefully and see what we can cook up for our next author visit. What do you think, Sonja?"

Sonja was looking through the digital pictures they had taken of Mavis Harmon. "I think I should put these up on the internet . . ." Before she could say anything else, Grace began to cry. Cassie, who had been watching the sleeping child, brought her to Sonja.

Rose, Melissa, Joan, and Cassie told Sonja to tend to her daughter while they took care of cleaning up. Sonja stood at the doorway leading to her apartment for a moment. Four women she had known for only the briefest of time were busy in Libby's kitchen helping her. Friends. She could almost hear Libby's voice in their chatter. For an odd moment, Sonja was the happiest she had ever been in her life.

The feeling didn't last. Grace had a slight fever and was fussy through the night. A trip to the clinic the next morning revealed an ear infection.

"But I'm nursing her," Sonja told the woman assigned to her case. "I thought if I nursed her, she would be immune to stuff like this."

"Nursing is good, but there are no guarantees. First baby, I'm guessing?"

Sonja nodded and then headed out to pick up the prescription for Grace on her way home.

"My sweet baby . . . you don't even know what's happening, do you?"

"I'm going to see if Joan can come help out," she told Melissa. "I think I should keep Grace away from the coffee shop customers for a few days."

Grace's medicine caused her to sleep more than usual. With Melissa and Joan running the day-to-day operations, Sonja used the time to draft an article for the weekly, reporting on Mavis Harmon's talk and to promote the next one in October featuring Cynthia Ruchti. She designed a flyer to distribute. Melissa's classes at the university would begin in a couple of weeks, so she had tearfully given her notice to Sonja, promising to return for the October author visit.

"It's actually perfect timing," Melissa had said. "The talk is right during our fall break at school." Melissa always had a way of looking on the bright side.

Sonja hugged Melissa. "I'm going to miss you."

She planned a farewell party for Melissa. The young woman was more than an employee. She had become a friend.

Sonja planned the party for the last Sunday Melissa was in town. In addition to the group of believers who met each Sunday in the Upper Room for church, Sonja wanted to invite several of the "regulars" from the coffee shop as well. Fearful she would accidently leave someone out, she made a colorful standup trifold for each table announcing the farewell gathering.

"I figure I couldn't pull off a surprise party, anyway," she told Melissa as she placed the trifold on the tables.

Grace was feeling better. She was satisfied to lie in her play yard on the enclosed service porch watching the mobile or sit in the swing near the doorway of the kitchen. Joan dropped by more often now that Cassie had started college. When business was light, she would visit or help Sonja by keeping watch on Grace. When business was heavy, she would roll up her sleeves and work the kitchen. Sonja knew Joan was missing her own daughter. She welcomed the company and the help.

Sundays soon became the highlight of Sonja's week. She wasn't sure when it happened; but one morning after Melissa returned to the university, Sonja woke up and realized she couldn't wait for Sunday. Kevin's messages always seemed to have been written just for her. She knew that wasn't the case but was constantly amazed at how much of what he said applied to her own life.

When Kevin first drafted the proposal for the new church, he had called it Open Door Ministries. In its infancy, members had called it Kevin's Church or referred to it as "a home church." Now, most people in the area knew it simply as The Church in the Upper Room. Sonja had her own name for it. She called it the Matthew Ministry. Customers in the coffee shop picked up on it, and soon people called it the Matthew Ministry in the Upper Room.

"I didn't intend to rename the church," Sonja told Kevin one Sunday morning. "I just noticed that you often use passages from the book of Matthew for sermons."

Everything had been put back and cleaned up. It was September, so few customers made their way to the shop on a lazy Sunday morning. They started down the stairs.

"I guess I do rely heavily on Matthew," Kevin admitted. "When I was sitting in that jail cell, I studied all of the Gospels, but kept coming back to the Sermon on the Mount. The Bible I had been given was one where all of Jesus' words were written in red. That was the first big passage of His words I came across. I think I just wanted to hear what Jesus had to say."

"I remember the first sermon I ever heard you preach. You were talking about the mission of the church here, and you used a verse from Matthew chapter three, when John the Baptist basically told people they couldn't count on being saved from God's judgment just because they belonged to Abraham's line. You said, 'Everyone must make the decision for him or herself. You can't be born a believer the way you can be born an American.' Remember that? Just because my parents are Christians doesn't make me one. Melissa told me the same thing."

Kevin stopped on the landing and stared at Sonja. "Wow. And I sometimes wonder if people are listening."

"I'm listening." Sonja took a deep breath. "Do you have a few minutes?"

The two made their way to the now-empty dining room and sat down at a table in the corner. "I need to tell you something."

Could she do this? Share everything? Bare her soul? Could she look at him?

Slowly, Sonja began to share with this gentle man her own story. She left nothing out. She told him how she had been raised in the church. She told him she hadn't followed the teachings she learned as a child when she was in college, even though if asked, she would have said she was a Christian. She told him about her life in San Diego and her longing for her family. She told him about her Grandma Grace and her purchase of the coffee shop. And she told him about Damon.

Kevin listened. He didn't interrupt. Even when her voice broke, he didn't offer platitudes. Even when she paused to regain her courage, he didn't tell her everything was okay. Even though tears threatened to push their way down her cheek and she had to rub them away with the back of her hand, he listened.

When she came to the end of her story, he simply asked, "And now?"

Sonja needed to make a decision. Yet something held her back.

"Now what?" she asked. "Now, I have just told you everything. I'm a fake and a liar. I had a baby out of wedlock. Isn't that enough?"

Kevin smiled. He reached across the table and took her hand. "Who are you trying to convince you are unworthy of God's love—me or yourself? Sonja, God loves you. He has forgiven you each and every time you have turned your back on Him. He wants a relationship with you.

"Look, you have a GPS in your car, right?" At Sonja's nod, he continued. "You know where you want to go; but you know that left on your own, you might get lost. So, you trust that little bit of technology to get you to the destination you desire. When it says turn right, you turn right. No questions asked.

"God created you. He gives you excellent directions to get you to the place you long to be. Next to Him. I heard someone call the Bible a GPS: God's Plan of Salvation." Kevin handed her his Bible. "Here, take this. And like someone told me, make good use of your time." With that, he left.

Sonja owned a Bible. True, she hadn't been able to unearth it from her things in storage. She looked at the book in her hands. Kevin's Bible. Tentatively, she opened the front cover, halfway expecting to see a note from his lawyer or some artifact from prison tucked within the pages. Instead, she found an inscription from his brother. It read, "Brothers by blood, now brothers in Christ. Welcome to the family. Love, Keith." Keith was younger than Kevin. He was a soldier in Afghanistan—his third tour. He would be coming home in March. That's about all she knew about the man. Until now. Now she knew he was a believer as well.

Sonja flipped through the pages. *Where should I start? At the beginning? With something familiar?* Finally, she turned to the Gospels, starting with Matthew. She would have another hour before Grace would wake up, or customers started drifting in for a sandwich and coffee. She opened to the New Testament and began reading the lineage of Jesus.

CHAPTER 31

EVER SINCE HER VISIT WITH Margaret Atchinson before the author talk in August, something had been gnawing at her. As business would likely remain slow until the pumpkin festival, Sonja decided to close early on a Wednesday, pack what she would need for the baby, and visit Joe Davis. She needed to know if Judy had, indeed, returned to visit her father.

After carefully researching recipes and experimenting with a few filling concoctions, Sonja landed on a sugar-free cherry pie filling and did her best to make Joe a diabetic-friendly cherry kringle. Her efforts at producing the pastry by herself to this point had been awkward at best. She knew she lacked the light touch Melissa used in handling the delicate pastry. She trusted, however, that even though her kringle didn't look pretty, it tasted like the real thing.

As she drove, Sonja tried to think of how she could get the information she needed about Judy. She didn't want to ask Joe directly for fear of upsetting him. Grace sat happily in her car seat for the first several miles. Sonja could see her in a mirror she had attached to the visor for that purpose. As they crossed Sturgeon Bay, she noted her daughter was sleeping peacefully. She knew it would be less than an hour before they arrived at Happy Years. *Grace's schedule will be thrown off for the day, but it's worth it. I'm the one likely to lose sleep, not the baby.*

Sonja stopped at the nurses' station. Balancing Grace in her carrier, she had the diaper bag slung over her back and carried the kringle in a bag, along with a thermos of coffee in her other hand. Sonja approached the attendant. "I have a question." Once she had the young woman's attention, she continued, "I'm here to see Joe Davis. I know he's diabetic, so I made a sugar-free pastry for him. I just wanted to make sure that would be okay." Sonja flashed the sweetest smile she could muster.

The woman frowned. "I will have to ask my supervisor," she told Sonja. Sonja was prepared.

"Oh, I totally understand. And I brought cookies for the staff. You all do such a wonderful job here." She set the thermos and bag on the counter. She then brought up her secret weapon, lifting Grace's carrier up and setting it on the counter, so she could pull the cookies out of the bag.

"What a precious baby!" the attendant cooed. "She is so sweet. What's her name?"

"Grace. She'll soon be six months old," Sonja shared. "What's your name?"

"Liz. You know, like Liz Taylor. My mom was a big fan."

Liz talked about how sweet the baby was and started talking about her own children. She was hooked. Sonja pulled the cookies out of the bag. She had three small, white bags of cookies, a dozen in each. The attendant read the sticker on the bag.

"Oh, you brought cookies from Libby's Cuppa Joe! How wonderful! Mr. Joe talks about that place all the time."

"Really? Does he ever talk about his daughter, Judy?" Sonja asked tentatively.

"Are you Judy?"

"No, I'm Sonja. I just wondered if you ever met Judy. I mean, has she been by lately? I'd love to see her."

"Oh, I've never met her. She might come on weekends."

"Oh, I see. I'm only in town for today. Maybe you could get me her phone number."

"I'm sorry. I'm not allowed to give out phone numbers," Liz said.

Plan B. "I understand. But thank you, anyway. And I won't give him the kringle until you hear from your supervisor." Sonja picked up Grace.

"I think it will be okay. You said it is sugar-free, right?" Liz asked.

"Right. Uh . . . thanks," Sonja called over her shoulder as she headed down the hall toward Joe's room.

Joe was in bed. For a moment, Sonja hesitated. What was she doing here? Was he asleep? Should she leave a note?

She was mulling over her options when Joe opened his eyes. "Hello there!"

"Hi, Joe. I'm Sonja, from the coffee shop."

Joe felt around on the nightstand beside his bed for his glasses. Sonja moved closer, located the missing eyewear, and handed them to Joe.

"I know you!" Joe called out. "You're the little girl that bought the store."

"That's right. Are you feeling okay?"

"Had me a bout with pneumonia a couple weeks ago. I'm okay now, but it sure did leave me run-down."

She pulled the pastry from the bag. "I brought you some cherry kringle." She poured the man a cup of coffee.

"Oh, that sure smells good," Joe murmured.

"And I brought you a special visitor." Sonja lifted Grace from her carrier, so Joe could see her.

"Now, who is this?" Joe asked.

"Joe, this is my daughter, Grace. Grace. This is Mr. Davis."

Joe smiled broadly. "She sure is a pretty little thing, isn't she?"

"I think so." Sonja beamed.

The next few minutes, they talked about the kringle, the coffee shop, and Grace.

"Me and Libby had a daughter. She was beautiful, too. Named her Judy." Joe's eyes were moist.

"I know," Sonja told him. As much as she wanted to learn about Judy, Sonja was suddenly afraid to go down this road. She didn't want to upset her friend. "Well, we better get going," Sonja offered by way of changing the subject after a few minutes. "We have a long drive back."

She put Grace back in the carrier and put the lid on the thermos. She needed to get out of there quickly. The baby carrier in one hand and the thermos and diaper bag in the other, Sonja hastily walked down the hall, almost running into an older gentleman walking the other way. "I'm sorry."

Sonja stopped near the nurses' station to properly strap Grace into her seat and gather her thoughts. *I hope I didn't upset Joe.* She pushed the button for the elevator and waited.

"Oh, Miss!" a man's voice called to her. Sonja turned to see the man she had bumped into in the hall. As he neared, she realized he looked like a slightly younger, thinner version of Joe.

"I'm Joe's brother, George. George Davis." He put his hand out to meet her.

"Sonja Parker," she shared.

"Joe was talking about a little girl just visiting him, and he said something about a daughter. I thought maybe . . . well, it doesn't matter. You're the one who bought Libby's, right?"

"Right. I just came to see Joe and bring him some kringle. And I wanted him to meet my daughter." Sonja looked down at Grace, who was happily chewing on her pacifier.

"That was kind of you." He looked at the smiling baby in the carrier. "She's a cutie."

"Thank you. Mr. Davis, may I ask you a question? I'm not trying to be nosy, but has Judy been to see her dad?" Surely if anyone would know, it would be Joe's brother.

George looked down and slowly shook his head. "When he said something in there about you and that you had just left, I was hoping Judy had come back. That maybe you were her daughter or something. That's why I ran out here. You got a minute?"

George led the way to a corner of the mostly unoccupied common room, where they sat down. His account of Joey's accident and Judy's leaving revealed nothing Sonja didn't already know. She let him talk.

"Joe and Libby were broken. It took years for them to regain some sort of normal life. I remember Libby baking dozens of cookies for all the kids in Fish Creek for Christmas. And on their kids' birthdays, they started buying presents for other kids. I can't tell you how many kids learned to ride on bicycles Joe and Libby bought for them because they didn't have their own kids."

"Did they try to hire a private detective or anything?"

"They spent a small fortune trying to find Judy. It was bad. Libby always said Judy would come home when she learned to forgive herself.

She was sure Judy would just show up one day on the front step. I always hurt for her. For all of them really."

* * *

The journey back to Fish Creek was slow. Dark clouds threatened rain. Sonja wanted it to rain. She wanted the whole of Wisconsin to have itself a big, hard, long cry. She wanted to go back in time and shake Judy and tell her how much she was loved and how nothing she ever did or could do would change that love. Her parents had forgiven any role she had played in Joey's death. Why couldn't she see that? Why couldn't she see that by not accepting their forgiveness and love, she wasn't just punishing herself, she was hurting them, too? *Like me, God?*

CHAPTER 32

THE ADVOCATE **RAN THE STORY** Sonja wrote about Mavis Harmon's author talk almost word-for-word. At the end of the story, Sonja included information about the author talk scheduled for the second week of October. Two weeks before the event, she wrote another article talking about the book, giving a biographical sketch of Cynthia Ruchti. She pulled the information from the internet. As Sonja reread the article, she found she was really looking forward to meeting the writer in person.

The second article proved to be a success. She distributed flyers to the area resorts, just as she had done the first time. This time, she also posted the colorful flyers in all of the Egg Harbor stores and restaurants. Since the pumpkin festival was centered in the Egg Harbor area, she wanted to make sure she created a buzz about the Meet-the-Author event at Libby's Cuppa Joe in Fish Creek.

"Maybe you should have gone into marketing," Rose told her when she looked over the reservation list. "You're going to have a full house!"

"I know. Can you believe it? I can have forty in the Upper Room, and we're almost there."

"Then what will you do?" Rose asked.

"Tell them we're booked, I guess. Any other ideas?"

"Maybe you could move the book signing part downstairs and make it more of an open house kind of thing."

"I thought about that, but, no. I think it is special to be part of an intimate group like that."

The menu was set. Melissa was coming Wednesday evening and was planning to stay until after church on Sunday. Although the customer traffic slowed this time of year, Sonja was busy baking pumpkin muffins with streusel topping for the large number of patrons she expected during the festival.

Grace was beginning to coo. She seemed to be playing with the sounds her mouth could make. Sonja talked to her through the day and read her books at night. She envisioned a time when she and Grace would be able to sit at the table and have quiet conversations at the end of the day. Grace would tell her of her school day, and she would share the goings-on of the coffee shop.

Joan laughed out loud when Sonja described her imagined conversations of the future. The two were sitting on Sonja's front porch, enjoying a cup of tea and a slice of double lemon pound cake.

"What?" Sonja asked, somewhat offended.

"I'm sorry." Joan chuckled. "It's just I know how those conversations go. You'll say, 'How was school?' And Grace will say, 'Fine.' And then you will tell her you baked six dozen cookies, and she will roll her eyes. End of conversation."

"You are very cynical, you know that? But what amazes me is how you perfectly described many conversations I had with my own mother."

The two women laughed and shared all the silly ideas they had about being a mother before they had children.

"It may not have happened to you yet," Joan warned, "but one day you will hear your mother's voice come out of your mouth. Just be glad you had a sweet mom."

"What was your mom like?" Sonja poured each of them another cup of tea.

"My mom? Well, she yelled a lot. She was never a happy person."

"But you're the total opposite. And I have never heard you yell at your children. You always explain things to them. I think you're such a good mom."

"Thanks, but that is more because of my Father. The Heavenly One. I try to parent in a way that pleases Him. Craig taught me that."

"I bet Libby was a good mother," Sonja mused.

"I'm sure she was. I never knew her children, but I've heard stories. And I know the kind of people she and Joe were," Joan agreed. "I know she always tried to do what was right. She loved people, and she loved to read. I know she would be pleased with the author visits."

"I think I would have liked her."

"She would have loved you. Are you ready for your author visit next week?"

Sonja was about to answer when her cell phone rang. "Speaking of mothers, that's mine. Sorry, I should take this." Sonja swiped her phone. "Hey, Mom!"

She started toward the door. She would go inside to speak to her mother. She didn't get far. "What? When?" Then, "No, I'll be there. I'm on my way." Click, and the phone was off.

"My dad had a heart attack!"

* * *

Sonja was just south of Green Bay when her phone rang again. Hesitant to answer because she was driving, yet anxious to answer because it could be news about her father, Sonja pulled over to the side of the road. Fortunately, traffic was light. Sonja fished in her purse for the ringing instrument.

"Hello?" she gasped without looking at number.

"Sonja? It's Kevin. Are you okay?"

"I was going to call you. I gave the keys to Joan Linder for you."

"I know. Joan called me. She told me about your dad. I would have driven you to Kenosha."

"Thank you for that, but I had to get on the road." Sonja switched the phone to speaker and slid it under her bra strap for hands-free talking. *I really need to get one of those earpiece things.*

"I'm sorry. Are you driving and talking now?"

"Uh . . . it's okay. I'm hands-free." A quick look in the mirror, and she was on the road again. Grace was fast asleep.

"Well, if you need me . . . I mean, I've been through this with my own dad. I understand. What hospital is he in?"

"It's called United," Sonja called out to her shoulder.

"I'll call later. I just wanted you to know that if you need me . . . " Kevin's voice trailed.

"I'll call. Kevin? Please pray for him."

"Praying as we speak. Be careful." Click, and the call was over.

The sun was shining, which helped. Grace was asleep. Kevin was praying. Sonja allowed herself to think her father would, indeed, be okay. The drive seemed longer than usual, and she met with a deluge of traffic just as she entered Milwaukee. Grace woke up and began to cry. The sun was coming in on her. *I should have put that sunshade in the window for her.* She made her way into the right lane and toward the exit. She needed gas anyway. Grace continued to cry. When did she eat last? Sonja honestly couldn't remember. She tried to regroup. As much as she needed to get to her parents, she needed, even more, to take care of her daughter. She pulled into a combination gas station, fast food restaurant.

"First things first," Sonja told Grace. She slipped into the restroom, covered the baby changing table with one of Grace's cotton blankets, and changed the baby's diaper. From the insulated container, she pulled a disposable plastic bag with milk she had pumped a few days earlier. Sonja held the bag under the hot water for a moment to warm it, then left the dingy room to feed her daughter. She sat in the bright lights of the fast food area, poured the milk into a bottle, and offered it to Grace. At first, the baby was reluctant to suck from the bottle; but once the milk was flowing, she settled into a rhythm. *Why is Grace taking longer than normal to eat? Maybe because I'm so upset.*

The frustrated mother pulled out her phone as Grace sucked away at the bottle. Annette had said she would call as soon as she knew anything more. And she had. "Missed Call" flashed on the tiny screen. A quick look at the time stamp revealed her mother had tried to call her only a few minutes prior.

She looked at the face of her daughter happily sucking at the bottle. "I probably couldn't hear Grandma's call over your crying." She hit the redial button.

Two rings later, Sonja was pleased to hear her mother's voice. Annette sounded tired but less anxious than she had been on the phone before. "They did a stress test and decided to do an angiogram. The cardiologist came out a few minutes ago. He showed me the pictures. You can see the blockage. The doctor said they are going to do angioplasty. That's where they put a balloon-type thing in the artery to push it open. If that doesn't work, they will have to put in stents. They won't know more until they do the procedure."

The language was foreign to Sonja. She wanted to know what all of it meant but instead asked her mother, "Are you okay? Are you alone?"

"I'll be okay, sweetie. Pastor Mark is here and Lois from church. Where are you?"

"I'm in Milwaukee. I had to stop to feed Grace. I'll be there as soon as possible."

"Just be safe."

It was good to hear her mother's voice. Knowing the doctors had a plan and were taking care of her father should make her feel better. She hadn't cried before. She didn't have time. Now, the tears flowed.

"Please, God, please. Please make my dad okay. Please help the doctors, and don't let anything go wrong."

Grace finished eating. Sonja looked over the lighted menu posted above the cashier at the restaurant. Nothing sounded good. *I must not be hungry.* "How could I even think about food with your grandpa in the hospital, Grace?"

The baby-safe sunshade now in place and Grace happily strapped in her car seat, Sonja made her way back onto the highway. Traffic here was a little better. Sonja estimated she could be at the hospital in a little over an hour. She was moving along at a steady pace through the easternmost part of Milwaukee; but south of the city, the traffic slowed once more, coming nearly to a stop more than once.

Sonja had never used her GPS to make the trip to Kenosha. She didn't need it. Now, however, she quickly typed, "United Hospital Kenosha" in the alternate route feature. It took a few minutes to complete the satellite connection. The Interstate 94 route she was on popped up on the screen. Traffic was once again at a standstill. Sonja touched the icon on the screen requesting an alternate route. There were two. Both required a few more miles.

Creeping along until she finally reached the exit, Sonja left the multilane highway. A turn took her back under the traffic-laden highway toward a rural road. She drove the eastbound country road for a while until her GPS directed her to turn south, then east again. Eventually, she found herself in familiar territory. She was near Racine, now southbound on Highway 31. The road would be known as Green Bay Road as she neared Kenosha. It would take her south and only a half mile or so away from the hospital.

"You did good, Gladys," Sonja said, patting the GPS with feigned affection. *What was it Kevin had said about the GPS?* She couldn't remember.

CHAPTER 33

"**THINK ABOUT THE SPRING IN** a ballpoint pen," Dr. Karros stated. "A stent looks something like that. We put it in the artery, and it holds the artery open so the blood can move through it unobstructed."

The cardiologist explained he had to put two stents in Daniel's heart. He showed Annette and Sonja on a model where the obstruction occurred. Sonja listened with interest and tried to remember everything he was saying. She knew her dad would want to know exactly what the doctor had done. Annette was just relieved the first words Dr. Karros had said when he entered the room was that Daniel had come through the procedure beautifully and was in recovery. She was also happy her daughter and granddaughter were finally there beside her.

Pastor Mark left after hearing the initial good report, promising to return in the morning to check on Daniel. Lois offered to watch Grace for a bit and had taken her on a walk outside in the stroller.

"How long until we can see him?" Annette asked.

"Not long. Someone will come out to get you as soon as he's in recovery."

"And he'll be okay?" Sonja asked.

"We generally have great success with this procedure. There was minimal damage to the heart itself. We'll talk about eating and stress management down the road, but there is no reason to think he can't live a long and happy life. This is a wake-up call. He's lucky." Dr. Karros shook their hands and left.

Forty minutes later, a nurse came out to tell Annette and Sonja they could come in for a few minutes, even though, in the nurse's words, Daniel was still "groggy and foggy." Lois, having returned with Grace, offered to stay with the baby while Sonja accompanied her mother.

Only later that night, as Sonja climbed into her own bed in her parents' home, did she realize the sacrifice Lois had made for her friend, Annette. She had taken off of work and given her entire day to sitting with Annette, getting her food and drink, and taking care of Grace, so Sonja could tend to her mother and father. It had been a long day. A frightening day. Sonja relived the day with the phone call, the long drive, the traffic jam just below Milwaukee, the waiting room, her father hooked to machines.

A thought, a revelation of sorts, nagged at her tired consciousness. It was something about the traffic jam. The elusive notion stayed just below the surface of clarity until she finally drifted to sleep.

The next morning, Annette and Sonja poured over the pamphlets a nurse in the cardio unit had given them regarding Daniel's future care.

Sonja held the dietary plan in her hand. "No sodium, no cholesterol, no fat? How about no taste? I'm thinking Daddy will never be able to eat anything I cook again."

"I know. I'm going to have to learn how to cook all over. And no more pizza nights. He's not going to like this."

The two women settled on a plan. Sonja's friend, Gina, agreed to watch Grace in the afternoon. That should be easy enough, since the baby took a nap from one-thirty to three-thirty or so every day. Annette intended to be at the hospital at eight o'clock when she would be allowed to go into the cardiac unit and visit her husband. Sonja would come around noon, as soon as she dropped Grace off at Gina's house, so her mother could eat lunch and not worry about Daniel being alone. Both were anxious to see Daniel, learn of his progress, and find out when he would be coming home.

Sonja cleared the cereal bowls she and her mother had used, while Annette got ready to leave. With luck, she would have another hour or so before Grace woke up. She needed to make a few phone calls. She made the list. She had promised to call Joan with an update. She would call Kevin, too. She couldn't remember if she had promised to do that or not; but he was praying for her dad, so he should get an update as well. Melissa was next on her list. *Although, Melissa may have an eight o'clock class.* Melissa moved to the top of the list.

The author visit was next week. Depending on how Daniel was faring, Sonja may or may not make it to the event. She wanted to be there. *A Door County Christmas* had proven to be a wonderfully engaging book. Though each story was well-written, Sonja paid particular attention to "The Hearts Harbor," since the story's author was soon to be the guest at Libby's Cuppa Joe. She was looking forward to the author visit; but if she was needed here, here is where she would stay.

"Melissa? It's Sonja."

"Sonja," came a groggy voice.

"Sorry to call so early, but I have a problem." Sonja explained about her dad's heart attack. "The thing is, I may not be back in time for the author visit. Joan's keeping everything sort of running for me now; but this time of year, it's mostly locals and no problem. I was hoping you might take the lead for the author event. It's sold out, and everything's ready. I even decorated an artificial Christmas tree for the event with little coffee cup ornaments and red bows all over the branches. It's tucked just inside the door in the storage closet in the Upper Room."

"Of course, I'll do that. And don't worry. I'll pray for your dad. And you. I really miss you and Grace."

The call to Joan was brief. Joan assured Sonja all was well with the store and, like Melissa, promised to pray for Daniel.

Sonja saved her call to Kevin for last.

"The doctor says he'll be okay. He called it a 'wake-up call.'"

"That's good news. I've been praying," Kevin replied.

"I could feel it," Sonja told him, much to her surprise. She only then realized she actually could feel the prayers being offered on her father's behalf.

"I'm glad you had a safe trip. I saw on the news a semi-truck had overturned on Southbound 94, and I was afraid you would be caught up in that mess."

All of a sudden, the thought Sonja had toyed with the night before came to her. "Kevin, you know how I teased you about preaching from the book of Matthew? Well, I've been reading it for myself." Sonja could almost hear Kevin smile over the phone. "Anyway, remember that part about the narrow path and the wide path? This may be too obvious; but I was in that traffic jam, and I pulled out the GPS. It directed me to an alternate route. It took me off the wide, well-traveled but congested interstate and onto small country roads. I got to the hospital with no problem. It made me think of that verse. Is that silly?"

"Not at all. It's actually a great illustration. Maybe, if you let me, I'll use it sometime. When we follow God, it may not be the popular, well-traveled route; but we arrive at the destination He intends for us. It's called trusting Him." Kevin was in preacher mode. Sonja could tell by his tone of voice. This time, she was the one sending a smile across the line. She didn't interrupt. He finished his discourse with an apology. "Uh, sorry. I guess I get a little excited when I talk about God."

"And you apologize for that? Hmm . . . doesn't sound like you. Anyway, Grace is beginning to stir. I'll call this evening after I get back from the hospital. Uh, I mean if you want me to."

"I want you to. Uh, maybe . . . "

"Yes?"

"Uh, well . . . later."

"Later."

CHAPTER 34

DANIEL SAT IN HIS RECLINER and reluctantly allowed Annette and Sonja to fuss over him the first two days he was home from the hospital. "I don't like being treated like a baby."

"The doctor said to take it easy, Dad."

"When are we going to eat? I'm hungry."

"Mom's fixing dinner now, Dad." Sonja pulled her mouth tight.

Annette put the plated food on the table. "Sorry I took so long, Daniel. Did you want to offer the blessing, Sonja?"

Sonja shook her napkin and placed it on her lap. "Uh, no, you go ahead, Mom."

Annette's blessing for the food was barely audible. Something about having patience with each other and hoping the food tasted good. She looked up and flashed a big smile to Daniel. "I tried one of the recipes in the book they gave me at the hospital," Annette said. "And it took me forever at the grocery store. I read every label. The doctor said to cut down your sodium intake. And cholesterol. And fat."

"And taste." Daniel put down his fork. "What is this, anyway?"

"Tofu meatloaf. The book says it's delicious."

"Tofu? Isn't that some kind of soybean stuff? How can that be a meatloaf? A meatloaf has meat in it."

The green beans "needed salt."

The brown rice "needed something."

The salad dressing was "awful."

"I'm not trying to complain," Daniel said.

Too late. Annette retreated to the bedroom in tears.

"I'm sorry," Daniel told Sonja.

"Hey, don't tell me."

The next day, Sonja picked up a salt substitute at the store for her dad, but even that didn't satisfy him. He was, however, in a more congenial mood.

Annette prepared a baked chicken and mixed vegetables. Daniel coated everything with pepper, making the no-salt, no-cholesterol, no-fat foods somewhat palatable.

By day four, Daniel said he was tired of sitting, tired of taking it easy, and tired of being babied. He talked Annette into going out for a short walk.

"I'm supposed to get some exercise," he complained. "If I stay in here day after day, I'll go nuts."

Sonja had missed the author talk. She hadn't talked to Kevin or anyone else in Fish Creek for two days. As her parents went out for their walk and Grace slept peacefully in her portable crib, Sonja dialed Melissa's cell.

"Cynthia Ruchti was fantastic!" Melissa giggled over the phone. "It was so great. She talked some about her writing, and she answered questions; but Sonja, honestly, it was almost like a worship service. She was so filled with love for Christ, it just poured out! I wish you could have been here."

"Me, too."

"She had copies of her books, and she signed a copy of her newest novel for you. Do you want me to read what she wrote?" Without waiting for an answer, Melissa continued, "She wrote, 'I was thrilled, thrilled, thrilled to spend the afternoon at Libby's Cuppa Joe. My thoughts and prayers are with you and your family.' And she prayed for your dad right here. It was such a great afternoon."

The enthusiasm in Melissa's voice warmed Sonja's heart. She thought once the author visit was over, the last big event of her season, she would feel free to stay here with her family. But strangely, she found herself as restless as her father. Sonja longed to go home. Her dad was on the mend. She would be able to return to see him frequently in the coming months, now that the high season was over. But for now, she needed to go home.

"Tell Joan and, uh, everyone that I hope to get home soon." The realization that she thought of Fish Creek as home and that she wanted to stay there through the winter surprised Sonja. A plan to open for breakfast for the locals in the off-season was taking shape. *I could limit the days and hours I'm open, so I can still spend time with Mom and Dad. Except on Sundays. Where did that come from?*

The church. Sonja realized she didn't want to stop having the church at Libby's. It was just beginning to build momentum. But the welfare of the church wasn't her primary motive. Something else was happening. Something inside her. A seed of faith, planted long ago by her parents and grandparents, was beginning to take hold and grow. Sonja liked the feeling. She didn't want to lose it.

Sonja pulled Kevin's Bible from her satchel. Quickly, she again found the verses about the road. It was easy to locate. The Bible she was reading had subheadings scattered throughout the text. This one read, "The Narrow and Wide Gates." It was in the seventh chapter of Matthew.

"Enter through the narrow gate. For wide is the gate and broad is the road that leads to destruction, and many enter through it. But small is the gate and narrow the road that leads to life, and only a few find it." She read on. "The Parable of the Sower" in chapter thirteen caught her eye.

> 1 That same day Jesus went out of the house and sat by the lake. 2 Such large crowds gathered around him that he got into a boat and sat in it, while all the people stood on the shore. 3 Then he told them many things in parables, saying: "A farmer went out to sow his seed. 4 As he was scattering the seed, some fell along the path, and the birds came and ate it up. 5 Some fell on rocky places, where it did not have much soil. It sprang up quickly, because the soil was shallow. 6 But when the sun came up, the plants were scorched, and they withered because they had no root. 7 Other seed fell among thorns, which grew up and choked the plants. 8 Still other seed fell on good soil, where it produced a crop—a hundred, sixty or thirty times what was sown. 9 Whoever has ears, let them hear."

Sonja closed the book softly. Her mind jumped to the summers she spent with Grandma Grace and Grandpa Jim on the farm. She remembered the year they expanded the vegetable garden, and she helped them clear the land of rocks and weeds.

I'm like that garden. My parents planted seeds of trust and hope and faith. Perhaps they hadn't taken root in her at all. Perhaps she needed to get rid of the rocks and weeds in her own life first.

Grace began to stir in the portable crib. Sonja knew she needed more time to mull this over, but her daughter would soon be awake and hungry. Sonja fixed herself a sandwich and poured a tall glass of cold milk. She could eat while Grace nursed. She would tell her baby what she was thinking about over lunch. One thing Sonja had learned in the last few months was that Grace was a good listener while she was busy nursing at her mother's breast.

CHAPTER 35

BY FRIDAY, DANIEL WAS BARKING orders over the phone to his crew. "This is frustrating," he told Sonja. "I'd be much better off if I could do something. Anything."

"What did the doctor say?"

"I don't care what the doctor said. I know myself. I know I can't sit here twiddling my thumbs."

"I just don't want you to overdo," Annette told her husband.

"I'm not going 'to overdo,' as you put it. But I'll feel a lot better if I can keep an eye on things." Daniel put his hands on his wife's shoulders. "Look, I'm not going to do anything to put myself back in the hospital, Annette," he told his wife sincerely. "I intend to be around for a long time. I want Grace to know her grandpa. But sitting around all day is killing me."

"And you'll eat right?"

"I'll eat right."

"And only half days, right?"

"I'll work only half days until the doctor gives me the all-clear."

"You have your follow-up appointment in two weeks, Dad. You could wait until then. I mean you're busy in the fall, but nothing like it is in the spring, right?"

"Sonja, I have a lot of fall projects. I'd just feel better knowing everything is running smoothly. You, of all people, understand, don't you?"

"Like the coffee shop."

"Exactly like the coffee shop."

Annette called the cardiologist's office and left a message with the receptionist. The doctor called back about an hour later, spoke briefly with Daniel and then with Annette. After the conversation, Daniel announced he would return to light office work the next day.

"The doctor called this a wake-up call," she told Sonja. "I have to trust your dad to know his own body and to do what he needs to do to take care of it. Walking on eggshells is no way for Daniel Parker to live his life."

Instead of the traditional Friday night pizza, Sonja and Annette made a heart healthy chicken taco that was spicy and good. Daniel enjoyed it so much, he declared Fridays "taco night" from that point on.

"Hey," he laughed when his wife and daughter acted surprised at his flexibility in the matter. "People change. We all have different experiences in our lives that shape us and change us. Me? I just go for the big stuff like a heart attack!"

Sonja went to bed that night thinking about her father's words. Though spoken in jest, there was truth in them. Grace was sleeping peacefully in her portable crib at the foot of Sonja's bed. "You were a big change in my life," Sonja whispered to her sleeping child.

She climbed into the bed of her youth and pulled the quilt up around her. Grandma Grace made the quilt for her tenth birthday. Sonja traced the pieces of triangular-shaped fabric making up the colorful star patterns on the quilt with her finger. A few were cut out of remnants of material from dresses Grandma Grace had sewn for Sonja. Others were fragments of old play clothes and school clothes. Rags, really. Each star was sewn into a square, and each square was blocked with the same material Annette used to make the pink flowered curtains in Sonja's room.

As an adolescent, Sonja appreciated how the quilt matched the curtains. She took delight in pointing out to friends spending the night, the print that had been a favorite blouse or the blue flowered material that had once been an Easter dress. Now, though, as she lay in the soft light of her bedside lamp, Sonja studied the quilt more closely. It was beautiful. Prettier than any single piece of fabric that had gone into its making.

In the still night, Sonja lay in her bed weeping. This was what Kevin had shared with her. This was the message her parents had spoken of. This was what her grandmother wanted her to know. *God can take the torn and fragmented pieces of my life and create something new.*

"Now what, God?" Sonja whispered into the night. "Without You, I am a spent, worn-out rag. With You, I am a beautiful and useful quilt. That's what I want, Lord. No more doubt. I want to give myself over to You completely and have You make me into who You want me to be."

Rays of sunlight streamed across the quilt when Sonja awoke the next morning. Grace was awake, lying quietly in the autumn sunlight. Sonja sat up and took in a deep breath. The air in the bedroom was cool, but not cold. It was a sign of the changing of seasons. The cool air seemed to cleanse her body and awaken her mind. The revelation of God's love and plan for her life was as real in the morning light as it had been last night as she had finally drifted into a deep and restful sleep.

Throwing her covers aside, Sonja virtually jumped into her clothes, changed Grace's wet diaper, and with her daughter in her arms, made her way downstairs to the kitchen. Daniel and Annette were sitting in the kitchen engaged in quiet conversation.

"Didn't mean to interrupt," Sonja murmured as she entered the room.

Daniel looked up from the table. "Not interrupting at all! We were trying to be quiet, so you could sleep."

Sonja settled Grace in her seat and slipped into the bathroom. By the time she returned, Grace was no longer in the carrier but snuggled in her grandfather's arms.

"I'm making you a veggie omelet," Annette said as she set about chopping green peppers. "I just made one for us but didn't know when you would be waking up."

"They're really good, too," Daniel admitted. "Even if they are made out of egg whites. I think your mom is having fun with this new cooking challenge."

"It's a work in progress," Annette agreed.

"So am I," Sonja said solemnly. "I'm a work in progress."

Daniel started to make a joke; but Annette stopped him, sensing their only daughter, the mother of their granddaughter, had something important to tell them.

For the next half hour or so, Sonja shared with them how she had never truly given herself over to God. "Oh, I knew all the right words to say and could sing all the songs. The thing is, I never fully committed myself to God. Kevin says you're either all in, or you're all out. I sort of pretended to be a Christian." Sonja studied the faces of these two people she loved. "I don't mean to hurt you or disappoint you."

Annette touched her daughter's arm lightly. Daniel shifted his eyes to meet Grace's. He extended his hand to his granddaughter, who grabbed his finger with a little laugh.

"You don't seem all that surprised."

Annette smiled. "You'll find you sometimes know your child better than she knows herself."

Sonja leaned back in the chair. "I guess. Anyway, I've been reading the Bible. And I've been thinking a lot about, well, everything. Maybe Daddy's heart attack was a wake-up call for me, too." She told them about the parable of the sower and how, somehow, she knew she fit into that picture. And she told them about the quilt.

"Sweetheart, this is an answer to my prayers," Annette said.

Daniel reached for her hand. "Our prayers. And, honey, I want you to know I'm here for you. And if it means living on tofu burgers for the rest of my life, I'll be here for you."

Grace began to fuss, and the immediate need to feed the baby overshadowed the moment. Though not entirely.

"Grace, you have a new mama this morning. And I think you're going to like her," Sonja breathed into her daughter's ear.

CHAPTER 36

DANIEL ANNOUNCED HE DIDN'T REALLY want to go into the office after all. He, Annette, Sonja, and Grace drove to a park near Lake Michigan and spent the morning walking, talking, and reminiscing.

"I think now that your dad is on the mend, I should get back to my classroom," Annette told Sonja. "I need to spend some serious time getting my lesson plans together."

"Isn't it funny, Mom, how we feel as though we never have time to slow down? But when we're needed, we take the time; and nothing really falls apart the way we think it will. I mean, your students are probably okay; and the coffee shop did fine without me."

"We're not as indispensable as we'd like to think we are, are we?" Annette stopped walking and looked toward the shore. Daniel was standing on a large rock overlooking the water. "Yet, I don't know what I'd do without him. Maybe your dad's indispensable. At least to me."

Sonja let go of the stroller and gave her mother a hug. "I know what you mean. And whether I'm needed or not at the coffee shop, I think I better get back there."

Sonja fixed a light salad for their lunch, while her mother worked on the lesson plans. "Monday will come quickly," Annette said.

After lunch, Daniel attended to Grace. Sonja packed her things.

"You understand, don't you, Daddy?" Sonja inquired. "I just feel this need to get back."

"If anyone understands, it's me," Daniel assured her. "But I'll sure miss you and this little one."

It was late when Sonja and Grace finally pulled out of the drive. Barring severe traffic or weather issues, Sonja was sure she would make it back to the coffee shop by dusk. She texted Kevin. "Coming home. Be there tonight. Have good news to share."

A short time later, he acknowledged her text. "Need to set up for chrch anyway. Look 4ward to seeing u." Sonja laughed out loud at Kevin's attempted texting shortcuts. It just wasn't like him.

The miles crept by slowly. Sonja yawned and rubbed her eyes. Grace was happy and comfortable for the most part. Annette once said Sonja was blessed to have a baby who was such a good traveler. *I wish Grace's mommy was a good traveler.* Sonja had to stop twice for Grace and once for gas. Just outside Sturgeon Bay, the car jerked hard to the right. She struggled with the steering wheel. Quickly, Sonja applied the brakes and managed to get the vehicle off to the side of the road.

A significant amount of rubber was missing from the right rear tire. Sonja released a deep sigh and opened the trunk. She set the box holding the portable crib on the pavement. Sonja shifted her suitcases to the side and began unloading the tire-changing tools under the carpeted compartment. She was trying to set up the tire jack when a patrol car pulled up behind her.

"Everything okay, miss?" the patrolman asked.

"I have a flat tire," Sonja answered wearily.

The patrolman called something into the radio on his shoulder, then took the tools from Sonja and expertly changed the damaged tire.

"You won't want to drive too far on the spare," he warned her. "And you'll need to take it slow and easy." By the time Sonja was back on the road, the sun was already beginning to settle in the western sky.

"I wonder how far is too far. What do you think, Grace? Should we try to make it home?" She decided to try to drive on to Fish Creek and let the local mechanic work on getting her a new tire there. She drove slowly up the highway. "God, please keep us safe," she prayed. Sonja's shoulders relaxed. She loosened her grip on the wheel. *So, that's what it feels like. That's what people mean when they say they have a sense of calm that comes with knowing God is listening.* "Thank You, God."

Darkness was closing in. Grace cooed from her seat in the back. "Grace, I need to tell you about your father. Your Heavenly Father." Sonja began telling her daughter about her own life. She told her how God loved both of them and was protecting them. She sang one of the praise songs she had learned in the Upper Room.

The night was black and void of moonlight by the time Sonja pulled into the drive leading to Libby's Cuppa Joe. Rather than pulling around to the back of the building, she decided to leave her car near the front, so the mechanic could pick it up easily. She unbuckled Grace's car seat and removed the baby carrier from the base. Swinging her purse and the diaper bag over her shoulder and carrying the baby carrier with her daughter sleeping peacefully in its cocoon-like interior, Sonja made her way to the front door. It was unlocked. Not surprising. Kevin had planned to come over to set up for church and was probably waiting for her to come home. She went through to the dining room and set Grace, carrier and all, on one of the tables before tossing her purse and the bag onto a chair. A light glowed from the stairway leading to her apartment.

A noise coming from the kitchen startled her for a moment. She turned, expecting to see Kevin. Instead, Sonja found herself face-to-face with a bearded man. Even in the shadows, he seemed familiar. Damon. Panic rose in her throat like a hard knot. She heard herself let out a little gasp.

"Well, hello there, gorgeous. Aren't you looking good?" Damon's voice was low and raspy. She could feel his eyes roaming her body. He moved closer, staring appreciatively at her full breasts.

"What are you doing here?" Sonja finally managed to say.

"Just came to pick up a little back pay," Damon snarled as he reached a hand to touch Sonja.

"No!" she shouted as she backed out of his reach.

At that moment, the front door opened. Kevin rushed in. "What's going on here?" he demanded. At the same time, Grace began to cry. Damon looked first to Kevin and then past Sonja to the baby crying in the carrier on the table beyond her.

"So, that's the way it is," he mumbled. "Better you than me, buddy." With that, he started toward the door, stopping only briefly to say something under his breath to Kevin about Sonja. She couldn't hear what he said. Only her name. But she could see rage in Kevin's eyes.

Damon was out the door and into the darkness of the night when Kevin raced after him. Sonja grabbed Grace up and held her close. Quickly, she moved to the front door and peered into the black abyss.

"Please, Lord, don't let Kevin do something foolish," she prayed. "Please protect him."

Though it was only a few minutes, not knowing what was happening made the span of time seem interminable. Sonja wondered if she should find her phone and call 911. There was a scuffle and some unintelligible words, and then the roar of a motorcycle coming to life and tearing through the darkened streets.

A moment later, Kevin emerged from the shadows and trudged up the steps to the coffee shop. "I wanted to break every bone in his body. But I didn't. I couldn't."

"I was praying for you," Sonja whispered.

"I couldn't. I saw his eyes. Grace's eyes. He's her father, isn't he?" Kevin asked quietly. Sonja only nodded. She stared down at the floor, shaking. Kevin drew her and Grace close. "It's okay. It's all going to be okay."

Tears pushed their way down Sonja's cheek as Kevin began praying. Sonja felt her shoulders relax as she leaned into him.

CHAPTER 37

GRACE SLEPT THROUGH MOST OF the prayer in her mother's arms, squirming only for a moment as Sonja nestled her back into the car seat carrier and sat down in the chair by the table. Kevin picked up a chair that had fallen to the floor.

"He doesn't know, does he."

It was more a statement than a question, but Sonja shook her head wearily. "No. I tried to contact him early on, but it was as if he disappeared. Then I sort of gave up."

Kevin sat down and took Sonja's hands. "And now? Would you tell him now?"

"I don't know what I'd do." Sonja looked into Kevin's eyes. "What if he tried to take her? He's unreliable. He's a liar and a cheat! How can I chance that?"

"I don't know. I don't have all the answers. I know it's scary, but somehow I think you need to tell him."

"I've thought about it. I just don't know. I don't want him to be a part of her life, Kevin!"

"Matthew chapter ten," Kevin said softly.

"What does that have to do with any of this?"

"It's the chapter I was working with for tomorrow's sermon. Jesus tells His disciples that there is nothing to fear. Nothing in this world to fear." Kevin drew in a deep breath. "I'm nervous about it, too. But something tells me we just have to trust God in this."

Sonja slipped her hand out of Kevin's and touched the side of the carrier. "My parents said about the same thing. I've thought about it; but even if I wanted to contact him, I wouldn't know where to start."

Kevin pulled a tattered wallet from his jacket pocket and laid it on the table. "Maybe this will help. He dropped it in our little scuffle outside."

As Sonja picked up the familiar canvas wallet, Kevin stood to leave. "Wait, Kevin. What would you do?" Sonja crossed the room to meet him halfway.

"Me? I really don't know. It's risky and I . . . well . . . I can't stand the thought of anyone hurting you . . . or Grace. Part of me—a big part of me—wants to protect both of you from . . . well, anything." Kevin looked down. "And anybody."

"Maybe a third party could contact him. A lawyer or something."

"Harris."

"Harris?"

"Harris Gambrol from church. He's a lawyer. Maybe he'd know how to handle this. I bet he could figure out a way to legally protect you and Grace in all of this."

Sonja sighed. "I know what he wants. He wants money. That's why he came tonight. He was looking for money."

Kevin put his arms around Sonja and drew her close. "Then that's what we'll give him. Whatever he wants. We'll make it happen."

"But Kevin . . . "

"Sonja, don't you know you mean more to me than any amount of money I could make in a lifetime?"

EPILOGUE: ONE YEAR LATER

GRACE SAT ON HER GRANDMOTHER'S lap playing with the buttons on her blouse as Kevin invited the congregation of regular attendees and visitors to stay a bit longer. The message he delivered was one of love and hope. Now, he introduced his mentor from the seminary.

Dr. James stood in front of a small table the group had used for serving communion. "I want to introduce you to my sweet wife." Dr. James motioned with his hand, and a small woman with salt-and-pepper hair stood up. "You know, she's special. She's put up with me for forty years." A few people laughed. "Marriage is like that. A process of give and take. Most people think marriage is a fifty-fifty proposition. But I can tell you, it is more about each person giving one hundred percent. That way, if one person falls short, the other is likely to make up the difference. The Bible says two become one.

"Kevin, my brother in Christ, has asked me if today I would do something very special at this church," the elder minister said. He motioned to Sonja to join them.

Sonja stood and walked toward the front of the group. The champagne-colored linen and lace dress she wore fell softly over her petite frame.

"Today, we are asking all of you to bear witness of a union formed this day between this man, my friend Kevin, and the woman God has prepared for him as a lifelong helper, Sonja."

A hush fell over the congregation. Even those who suspected the couple were in love had not expected a wedding on this day. Visitors to the church readily recognized the blessing they were about to experience. Sonja and Kevin had shared their plan with only a handful of close friends and relatives. Only a few people knew of the lengths to which Kevin had gone to assure Sonja was no longer threatened by Damon. The money. The legal tangle of paperwork. The search for Damon's family.

Gina came with her own little family from Kenosha, and Melissa arrived with a handsome young man she met at college. Fran sent her regrets, along with a big bouquet of roses in a crystal vase. Most of the friends in attendance were from Fish Creek and surrounding towns in Door County.

Rose walked to Sonja's side and handed her a fall bouquet of flowers. She stood next to her friend. Keith, Kevin's brother, joined them as Kevin's best man.

"Who gives this woman to this man?" Dr. James asked as the four turned toward him.

Daniel stood, smiling. "Her mother and I." Sonja smiled, too. She knew her father had been rehearsing his line for the past several weeks, afraid he would mess it up and ruin his daughter's special day.

Kevin repeated the vows with a sincerity that mesmerized the room. "I take you, Sonja, to be my wife. To have and to hold from this day forward, for better, for worse, for richer, for poorer, in sickness and in health; to love, honor, and cherish from this day forward and, thereto, I pledge to you my love."

Her heart was full of love for this man as Sonja repeated similar vows to Kevin.

Dr. James read through the Scripture they had chosen. "These are the words of Jesus regarding marriage. They can be found in the book of Matthew, chapter nineteen, verses four through six. *'Haven't you read,* he replied, *that at the beginning the Creator made them male and female,* and said, *For this reason a man will leave his father and mother and be united to his wife, and the two will become one flesh.* So they are no longer two, but one flesh. Therefore what God has joined together, let no one separate.'"

At Dr. James' prompt, Keith handed a gold band to Kevin. "With this ring, I thee wed," Kevin said has he slipped the band on Sonja's finger. Sonja took a matching band from Rose's hand. "And with this ring, I thee wed," she said. A single tear slid down Sonja's cheek. Her face hurt from smiling. "I love you, Kevin Hanson," she whispered.

"By the power vested in me by the state of Wisconsin," Dr. James stated, "I now pronounce you husband and wife." Kevin bent to kiss his bride, just as Grace clapped her hands and said something totally unintelligible. The entire room laughed.

Dr. James winked. "Well, as Grace said, and I was about to say, you may kiss your bride!" So, Kevin kissed Sonja again. This time, the entire room broke into applause.

"Ladies and gentlemen, I give you Mr. and Mrs. Kevin Hanson," Dr. James declared.

"And you are all invited to the reception downstairs!" Kevin announced.

The dining room of the coffee shop was filled with bouquets of flowers. A plate of wedding cookies, along with a variety of breakfast cookies, was the centerpiece for each table. A small, but very traditional, wedding cake adorned a table in the corner of the room. The cake was the effort of Joan and Cassie Linder; and although it appeared just a little lopsided, Sonja deemed it perfect. She and Kevin cut the cake and delicately, respectfully, fed each other a small portion.

"Your grandmother would have been proud," Annette said. "She always despised the way some young people smash the cake in the face of the one they just promised to cherish."

Melissa made sure the coffee pots were filled. Music she downloaded and named "the wedding mix" played softly in the background. Cassie and Joan wove through the room making sure everyone had all they needed. Gina, an amateur photographer, had offered her services as a gift, so she busily snapped shots of the guests and the bride and groom.

As she made her way around the room greeting each of the partygoers, Sonja looked toward the door where Melissa was greeting a newcomer. Sonja caught a glimpse of the woman standing in the doorway. She looked familiar. *Probably one of last summer's customers here for the pumpkin festival. Probably didn't know the coffee shop is no longer open on Sundays.* The woman was wearing a red sweater with the black silhouette of a Scottish terrier dog woven into it. Melissa was obviously inviting her to join the party.

"I was just looking for the owners," the woman was saying as Sonja approached. Her voice was soft. It quivered as she spoke. She seemed almost frightened. Sonja could see the woman was older than she initially thought. *Maybe in her fifties.* She was a bit on the plump side with short, curly, dark hair. Her features were hard, like those of someone who had struggled with life. A young man stood on the porch just behind the woman. He, too, looked strangely familiar.

"I'm Sonja," she said. "We just had a wedding. Please join us," the bride told the two newcomers. The woman took Sonja's extended hand as she edged her way into the entryway.

"Oh, thank you," the woman stammered, searching the room with her eyes. "But I don't want to interrupt." Her eyes came to rest on the antique curio cabinet Sonja had placed in the entryway to display the ornate tea set that once belonged to Libby. The woman hesitated. "I was just looking for Libby. Or Joe." Her eyes turned back to the gathering of people eating and talking in the main dining area before turning to Sonja and looking her in the eye. "My name is Judy. This here's my boy. Come here, Joseph."

Sonja's eyes widened with recognition. A smile spread across her face. "Judy, Joseph, come with me. Another of my very special guests arrived a few minutes ago from Green Bay." Sonja slipped her arm in Judy's and guided her toward the dining area. "I have a feeling you're going to make his day!"

BREAKFAST COOKIES

- 2 C. brown Sugar
- 1 C. white sugar
- 1 ½ C. cooking oil
- 2 t. vanilla

Cream together.

Add:

- 4 eggs.
- 4 C. flour
- 2 t. baking soda
- 1 t. salt
- 1 ½ C. oatmeal
- 4 C. cornflakes

Mix together well.

Drop by teaspoons on greased cookie sheet.

Bake at 350 degrees Fahrenheit for twelve minutes or until brown.

Yield: 8 dozen

Variations: Try adding pecans, caramel bits, raisins, almonds, butterscotch morsels, or any combination. Sonja found success with all of these. A friend of mine is going to add coconut. Give it a try. Be creative. Enjoy.

For more information about

Rebecca Waters

&

Libby's Cuppa Joe

please visit:

www.WatersWords.com
www.facebook.com/RebeccaWatersAuthor
@WatersAuthor
www.goodreads.com/author/show/8087383.Rebecca_Waters

For more information about
AMBASSADOR INTERNATIONAL
please visit:

www.ambassador-international.com
@AmbassadorIntl
www.facebook.com/AmbassadorIntl

If you enjoyed this book, please consider leaving us a review on Amazon, Goodreads, or our website.

CPSIA information can be obtained
at www.ICGtesting.com
Printed in the USA
LVHW081727080319
609995LV00015B/386/P

9 781620 208670